OF CATTLE AND MEN

First published by Charco Press 2023
Charco Press Ltd., Office 59, 44-46 Morningside Road,
Edinburgh EH10 4BF

Copyright © Ana Paula Maia, 2013
First published in Portuguese as *De gados e homens*
by Editora Record (Brazil)
English translation copyright © Zoë Perry, 2023

A CIP catalogue record for this book is available from the British Library.

ISBN: 9781913867492
e-book: 9781913867508

www.charcopress.com

Edited by Francisco Vilhena & Fionn Petch
Copy-edited by Fionn Petch
Cover designed by Pablo Font
Typeset by Laura Jones
Proofread by Fiona Mackintosh

LOTTERY FUNDED

Ana Paula Maia

OF CATTLE AND MEN

Translated by
Zoë Perry

CHARCO PRESS

For my dear grandmother, Maria Maia

es ist ja bloß ein Tier… nur ein Tier.
(They're only animals… just animals.)

Theodor Adorno

For the life of the flesh is in the blood.

Leviticus 17:11

Chapter 1

Edgar Wilson is leaning against the door of farmer Milo's office. His boss is bellowing down the phone, having learned to bellow from a young age, out in the pastures, where he'd had to fight off the calves just to get to the cows' teats. The office is nothing more than a narrow cubicle crammed next to the slaughterhouse's gut room.

'You wanted to speak with me, sir?'

'I do, Edgar.'

'Yes, sir?' says Edgar Wilson, taking off his cap and clutching it respectfully against his chest as he enters the office.

'I need you to go down to the hamburger plant to make a collection.'

'Who will slaughter the cattle, Senhor Milo?'

Milo scratches his head, burying his fingers in the curly, tangled strands.

'I'm short-staffed, Edgar. And Luiz is the only one trained in your job, but he's supervising the slaughter line today. Let me think...'

Edgar Wilson stands silently, awaiting the boss's decision. Not a single thought crosses his mind, as it is not his custom to seek solutions unless requested.

'There aren't any big shipments for slaughter today,' says Milo, pensively.

Nor is it Edgar Wilson's custom to fail to comply with what has been asked of him. Milo is a hardworking man, works fourteen-hour days. He is a fair boss in Edgar's eyes.

'Zeca's slaughtered a few times before, right?' asks Milo.

'Yeah, he has. But he keeps the animals awake. The cattle really suffer, Senhor Milo. Zeca's aim isn't good.'

Milo looks at the employee spreadsheet and their duties. He mulls it over.

'Zeca's on tripe right now, but he's all I got,' he mutters to himself.

'Sir, he keeps the cattle awake.'

'You already said that, Edgar. What can I do? It'll die at sticking anyway,' replies Milo, upset.

Edgar stands there, unruffled, his grey eyes on his boss. The phone rings. Milo answers and asks for a moment.

'Here's the invoice, Edgar. The address is written there. Grab the keys for the truck from Tonho and send Zeca over to speak with me.'

Edgar Wilson nods and takes the bill. Milo gets back on the phone. Edgar hesitates for a moment before leaving but goes through the office door and shuts it behind him. He walks down a fetid, dark corridor and turns right, into the stun box, where he spends most of his hours. The line of steer and heifers is long, as always. An employee opens the hatch and a steer that's already gone through inspection and bathing enters slowly, suspiciously, looking around. Edgar picks up the mallet. The steer comes up close to him. Edgar looks into the animal's eyes and caresses its forehead. The cow stomps one hoof, wags its tail, and snorts. Edgar shushes the animal and its movements slow. There is something about this shushing that makes the cattle drowsy, it establishes a mutual trust. An intimate connection. With his thumb smeared in lime, Edgar Wilson makes the sign of the cross between the ruminant's eyes and takes two steps back. This is his ritual as a stun operator. He poises the mallet and strikes the steer's forehead with pinpoint accuracy, resulting in loss of consciousness caused by cerebral haemorrhage. Collapsed on the ground, the cow spasms briefly until it goes still. Edgar Wilson believes there was no suffering. The animal now slumbers serenely, unconscious, as it's taken to the next stage by another employee, who will hoist it upside down and slit its throat.

Edgar signals for the operator not to let the next steer enter the chute. He goes to the gut room and calls for Zeca, who obeys his order immediately. Minutes later, Edgar watches with a heavy heart as the boy leaves Milo's office and proceeds, grinning, to the stun box. Zeca is an eighteen-year-old kid, he's troubled. He likes watching the animals suffer. He likes to kill. He is getting ready for the task when Edgar enters the box and cautions him:

'Put the animals to sleep, okay, Zeca? Don't let them suffer.'

Zeca picks up the mallet and waves to the operator to let the next cow in. When the animal is standing face-to-face with him, he strikes one poorly aimed blow, on purpose, and the cow, groaning on the floor, writhes in agony. Zeca swings the mallet and smashes the animal's head with two consecutive whacks, blood spraying onto his face.

'Like that, Edgar? He's asleep now, ain't he?' Zeca blinks hard several times and noisily sucks his teeth.

Edgar Wilson doesn't react to Zeca's affront. He turns around and walks to the bathroom, where he changes his clothes. He puts on jeans and a plaid button-down shirt. After getting the keys from Tonho, he goes to the pick-up truck, bemoaning the broken radio.

Since he'd stopped working in the coal mines, the only job he could get was with cattle, but what he really wants to do is work with hogs. He's always liked pigs. He hopes to get a job soon at a large hog farm just a few kilometres away.

His precision is a rare talent that bears a preternatural knowledge for handling ruminants. If the blow to the forehead is too powerful, the animal dies, and the meat will toughen. If an animal feels fear, the pH level of its blood rises, which makes the meat taste bad. Some slaughtermen don't care. Edgar Wilson prays for the salvation of the soul of each animal he slaughters and puts it to sleep before its throat is slit. He's not proud of what he does, but if someone has to do it, then let it be him, who has pity on those irrational beasts.

After the animals are quartered, they're sent to two hamburger plants or distributed to various meat packers, which send trucks to pick up loads of beef. Edgar Wilson has never eaten a hamburger, but he knows that the meat is minced, pressed, and flattened into a disk. After it's fried, it's placed between two slices of round bread and topped with lettuce, tomatoes, and sauce. The price of a hamburger is equal to ten cattle slaughtered by Edgar, since he's paid for each animal he fells. He has to kill over a hundred heifers and steers a day and works six days a week, taking only Sundays off. Production at the slaughterhouse is ramping up and they'll have to hire another stun operator.

Edgar Wilson must drive for almost an hour along a road that skirts the riverbanks. This river is where all the slaughterhouses in the area dump thousands of litres of blood and cattle viscera. The river flows into the sea, and so does the blood of these beasts.

By the side of the road, Erasmo Wagner is leaning against a bicycle with a flat front tyre. He sticks out his thumb from time to time but hasn't managed to get a ride. Most of the vehicles traveling on this road are heavy trucks, along with a few horse-drawn carts. Usually it's deserted, with its twisting turns and uneven asphalt.

Edgar Wilson pulls the pickup onto the shoulder. Erasmo Wagner places the bicycle in the bed, opens the passenger door and sits down next to Edgar, visibly grateful.

'Thanks for stopping. I got a flat.'

'Where you headed?'

'I work construction, down at the new hamburger plant.'

Edgar Wilson extends his right hand in greeting. The man reciprocates the gesture:

'Erasmo Wagner. At your service.'

'I work at Senhor Milo's slaughterhouse,' says Edgar Wilson.

'I know the one. What is it you do there?'

'I'm the stun operator.'

Erasmo Wagner rolls down the window the rest of the way and sticks his elbow out. A little further down the road, lulled by the warm and gusty wind, he starts to lament.

'Plenty of folks have died out here.'

The row of tiny crosses on the side of the road is endless. Death touches everything inside that perimeter, both on the road and in the contaminated river that cuts through the region.

Edgar Wilson lights a cigarette and offers one to Erasmo Wagner. Clouds gather, covering the sky, but even with the clouds there's no sign of rain.

'When's the plant ready?' asks Edgar Wilson.

'If there's no more delays, I reckon another two or three months.'

'This one's gonna be a lot bigger than the other one. You work on the other one?'

'No. I was doing time back then. Got out about a year ago.'

'Were you inside for long?'

'Longer than I'd intended. But I squared my debt and now I'm free to die, right here on this road, even. Which is a whole heap better than dying in jail.'

'To die a free man is to die a lucky man.'

On the road there are steep uphill sections where the pickup loses power, requiring Edgar Wilson to shift gears, manoeuvring the lever with difficulty. On the left side of the road, a small pasture holds a few head of cattle. The cows chew their cud and rest among the mountainous, larger-than-life termite mounds built atop the grass in the middle of the pasture.

'There's a good chance cattle farming round here will grow,' says Erasmo Wagner.

'Yeah, with another hamburger plant, they're gonna need more meat. Work down at the slaughterhouse should increase, too.'

'How many head you slaughter a day?'

'Depends on the load. Sixty, sometimes ninety. One time I slaughtered a hundred and seventy head in one day. By the end of the night, I couldn't feel my arms.'

'Yeah... the stench of death is all around us.'

Edgar Wilson agrees with a nod.

'You like your work there at the slaughterhouse?'

'I do. Sometimes I don't like dealing with all the blood and death so much, but... it's what I do.'

Erasmo Wagner takes a long drag and blows the smoke out the window. The warm, bitter wind disperses it.

'Somebody's got to do the dirty work. Other people's dirty work. Nobody wants to do that sort of thing. That's why God put guys like you and me on this earth.'

Edgar Wilson stares ahead as far as his eyes can see, to

the phantom line that separates road from sky. Just a line, one that can never be reached.

'The worst thing about slaughtering cattle is looking into their eyes.'

'What about 'em?'

'I don't know. You can't see a thing deep inside a bull's eye.' Edgar Wilson pauses uneasily. 'I keep looking, trying to make out something, but you can't see a thing.'

Edgar shakes his head and shrugs. He tosses his cigarette out the window and blows the remaining smoke from his lungs.

'What were you in for?'

'I killed an ol' son of a bitch. Was a son of a bitch his whole damn life.'

Edgar Wilson is briefly dismayed. Silence blankets their heads. These are the confessions of blood and death of those who have already been condemned. There are others like them on the side of that same road, both above ground and below it. The murmur of those who never returned echoes against the rocks, a lamentation, because when there is no one to pray, the rocks cry out.

They sit in silence for the rest of the trip. Erasmo Wagner thanks him for the ride a second time and, pushing his bicycle with the flat tyre, walks towards the plant.

As he continues on his way, Edgar Wilson's thoughts are fixed on the darkness of the ruminants' eyes, endeavouring to locate some small sign that might unveil the mystery. However hard he tries, his imagination casts no light: neither on the darkness of those unfathomable eyes, nor on the darkness that cloaks his own wickedness.

★ ★ ★

When he arrives at the hamburger plant parking lot, Edgar Wilson identifies himself to the security guard. After communicating with another employee over the walkie-talkie, the security guard opens the gate and wishes him a good afternoon. Edgar returns the greeting.

He parks the old, rusty tan pickup between two new trucks. He tucks his shirt into his jeans, combs his fair, wavy hair, grabs the invoice and enters the plant. A woman greets him with a forced grin and takes him to a bright, airy and clean office. Edgar sits in a leather chair and waits to be seen.

Ten minutes later, a man in a suit enters the office and sits down at the desk. Edgar gets up and holds out the invoice to the man, who seems both very busy and bored.

'Senhor Milo sent me.'

The man looks him up and down for a few seconds. Then he presses the button on the top of a glossy pen, seemingly finding comfort in that irritating little noise.

'Senhor Milo?'

'The owner of the slaughterhouse. Touro do Milo.'

'Oh, right, Milo... our supplier.' The man pauses. 'So, how can I help you?'

'I have an overdue invoice.'

'Are you his accountant?'

'No sir, I'm the stun operator.'

Federico is the man's name. Edgar Wilson can just make it out on the badge clipped to the breast pocket of his jacket.

'The what?' he asks, furrowing his brow.

'The stun operator.'

Federico feels it best to put a stop to their conversation. He's imagining the work that the man before him does, and he doesn't like thinking about it. He looks down at the rest of his lunch on the desk: a hamburger with spicy brown mustard and pickles.

'Give it here,' he says, signalling the invoice in Edgar's hand. He checks the document. He makes a call to another department, speaking softly so only a few words are intelligible. He hangs up the phone, straightens his tie and says:

'I'm going to cut you a cheque, okay?'

Edgar nods.

'It was a miscommunication here. Apologise to Senhor Milo for this little delay. And tell him that we really appreciate the meat he sends us here. Down the hall, on the left. You'll see a door with a sign that says accounting. Just hand that invoice to the young lady who'll be expecting you.'

'Yes, sir.'

Along the way, Edgar Wilson passes men wearing white coveralls, totally sterile. He's never been to a place as clean as this. It's so different from the slaughterhouse where he works and from the housing where he lives, cooped up with several other workers. Two enclosures, one for cattle and one for men, standing side by side. Sometimes the smell is similar. Only the voices on one side and the mooing on the other distinguish the men from the ruminants.

In the accounting office, a short woman wearing glasses takes the invoice and hands him a cheque. He stuffs it in his pocket and walks out. A shipment of hamburgers is being loaded onto one of the trucks. He lights a cigarette and, leaning against the pickup, watches the men at work. One of the cardboard boxes falls from a tall stack and crashes to the ground. Edgar crouches beside the box and looks at the contents. It looks tasty. One of the loaders offers him a box of burgers. He thanks him and climbs into his cab.

It's late afternoon by the time he gets back, the sun is setting between irregular tufts of clouds and the hue of the twilight sky resembles that of a pomegranate cut in half. The clouds have dissipated, and the sunset's reflection gleams in Edgar Wilson's eyes, which even on sunny days are a stubborn grey colour.

He parks the pickup in the slaughterhouse yard. The workday is over, and the only employees still around are the ones finishing cleaning up. Edgar Wilson walks into Milo's office and hands him the cheque. In the stun box he notices an excessive amount of blood and pieces of broken skull.

It's the hour of the cicadas' song. Night draws in, enveloping the heavens and engulfing the twilight. A few stars have already appeared. Edgar Wilson enters the shared washroom. He waits until Zeca is the only one still in the showers. With a mallet, the tool of his trade, he strikes the boy squarely on the forehead, leaving him on the ground in violent spasms and low moans. Edgar Wilson makes the sign of the cross before lifting Zeca's dead body and wrapping it in a blanket. Not one drop of blood was spilled. His work is clean. He dumps Zeca's body at the bottom of the river, with the blood and cattle entrails, which, like the river itself, will be carried out to sea with the current.

His duty done, he goes to the kitchen and fries up the burgers. Together with his co-workers, they eat the whole box in astonishment. Round and seasoned like that, they don't even look like they had ever been a cow. Not one glimpse of the unbridled horror behind something so tender and delicious.

Chapter 2

The man holds his breath and plunges his head into a water barrel. At first, the others stand around making jokes. They laugh. When a minute passes, they gradually fall silent until only the hum of the blowflies that feed on the remains of dead cattle is left. Old Emetério, the slaughterhouse's longest-serving employee, with his wizened mouth, impregnated by the scent of the rolling tobacco he smokes every day, opens his trembling yellow eyes wide when the stopwatch he's holding passes two minutes. Nineteen seconds later, Burunga's head emerges, purple from the lack of oxygen. He lets out a guffaw that shakes his heavy, flabby belly. The men cheer and whistle. The day before, he'd managed to stay under for a minute and thirty-four seconds. Burunga collects the betting money, a few coins the men had tossed into his straw hat, and hikes up his trousers that are constantly slipping down. He checks his total profit from the betting and, with a grin, sticks the money in his pocket.

'Son of a bitch. He did it again,' mutters old Emetério in his gravelly timbre, sounding as if his throat were sore. 'That bastard!'

'Told you he'd do it,' says Helmuth, arms crossed, sitting on the back of a pickup truck that hasn't run in over ten years.

'Didn't stop you from betting against him,' grumbles Emetério.

'But one of these days, old-timer, he ain't coming back up,' Helmuth says with a wink, clicking his tongue.

After the blood is drained and the hide removed, the animal, suspended by chains, gets pushed along a rail until it reaches Helmuth, the splitter, who uses a chainsaw to remove the head and split the carcass in half. He is the only one doing this job and can break down up to two hundred cattle a day. He usually wears a black helmet and gloves, for protection. It's a job that requires proper technique and care. At work, Helmuth is engrossed, and his dead-fish eyes make him look even more gormless, but just like a dead fish, his eyes never stop gleaming. They are black and shiny like the eyes of the ruminants. He's good at dismantling things, be it a car engine, a steer, a jaguar, or a house. He can tear down walls in just a few hours.

When he found out his wife was cheating on him and the child he was raising was his brother's son, he didn't go on a bender, he didn't demand an explanation, he didn't make threats or even attempt murder to restore his honour. He waited until his wife went to visit her parents in another town and spent all night swinging a sledgehammer against the walls of the house. The house he shared with Jaqueline had just been remodelled and was newly furnished. With the money Jaqueline earned as a maid in a family's home, she had invested in renovations and bought new furniture. Helmuth's money was for everyday expenses. When she found the house of her dreams, which, although simple, was just the size her heart desired, she resigned from her job to devote herself to making her own home.

Helmuth knocked down every wall of the house, smashed the tub, the toilet and the bathroom sink, the marble worktops in the kitchen, took apart the television, radio, and the refrigerator. He set the beds and the salmon-pink sofa on fire in the backyard, along with the dismantled armoire. He even dismantled the hair dryer, and when he opened it up, he removed the tufts of his wife's hair clogging the air outlet. He gathered his few belongings and left at dawn.

He went on to dismantle car engines in a mechanic's shop as soon as he arrived in another town, and not long after began slaughtering cattle at an abattoir, until he heard about the job opening to dismember them. And that is how he arrived at Senhor Milo's slaughterhouse, where he showed such impressive skill he was hired on the spot and allowed to live on site.

Old Emetério, still puzzled by Burunga's feat, gives Edgar Wilson a grilling.

'Don't look at me. I didn't bet a thing, old-timer,' Edgar replies.

Emetério grunts a few times, clears his throat and spits on the ground.

'Bastard! Better get back to work. Lunch break's over. There's a ton of offal waiting for me back in rendering.'

'You need to retire, old man,' says Helmuth.

Emetério shrugs and shuffles toward the back door, where he and all the other men, apart from Edgar Wilson, go inside to return to work. The old man proceeds to the rendering room, where products from the kill floor not intended for human consumption – offal, giblets, tripe and bone – are gathered. It's where they process waste

13

and produce bone meal and tallow. Every day he thanks God for allowing him to work this job, he still has some pep, despite his age. There are only four teeth left in his mouth, but that makes no difference when he's doing his job. He is as capable as he was thirty years ago. But for anyone outside of that slaughterhouse, he's as useless as the offal with which he works.

Edgar Wilson lights a cigarette and decides to stick around another five minutes, now alone and in silence. From where he stands, he watches the cows grazing in open pens, enclosed with barbed-wire fencing. He walks over to one of the pens and notices that some of the fences are no longer as taut as they should be.

In the late afternoons, when dusk begins to crack open ruddy crevices in the sky, like rifts in a volcano, the cattle leave their pasture and huddle in small groups under a tree. But today is overcast and the sky, instead of that crimson hue, will be rimmed in charcoal.

Edgar likes to watch the confined animals. Alone or in small groups, they keep the same pace when they chew or swish their tails. Cattle, every one of them, graze to the north, as they can sense the Earth's magnetic pull. Few know the reason behind this, but the people who work with cattle every day know they adhere to a code of conduct, and they all stand facing the same direction while grazing. This sort of harmony is unheard of in men.

A cow approaches Edgar. Slowly, she moves her flanks majestically while chewing a handful of grass. He strokes the animal's head. The cow has a brown mark on her forehead, in the shape of a teardrop. He will certainly remember her when they come face to face again.

He finishes his cigarette and turns to go back to the stun box. He sighs, sorrowful. It's his job, the only one keeping him alive. He looks back. The ruminants that are grazing quietly, standing in groups or alone – soon he'll come face to face with all of them: Edgar, the murderous beast himself.

At nightfall, blackness scoops up all traces of the day that has just gone by. Only the smell of blood and excrement remains. Some of the cattle are resting and most of the men have returned to their homes. Those who live in the dormitory usually gather at least once a week at a bar a couple of kilometres away. There they play pool, card games, drink and meet the perfumed prostitutes who are waiting for them, the cattlemen, as they're known. They all take cuts of meat as payment, but not just any piece. At the bar, a scale checks the weight. One service offered per kilo.

'Aren't you coming, Edgar?' asks Helmuth.

'Later, I'll be there later.'

'Don't be long. Old Emetério's on fire. He's gonna bag all the girls.'

Old Emetério bursts out laughing and slaps his thigh as if he were beating the dust from his trousers.

'I won't leave anything for you, Edgar,' says the old man with his withered mouth, excited.

Holding up his trousers, Burunga approaches Edgar Wilson.

'I haven't seen Zeca in days. You heard from him, Edgar?'

Edgar Wilson does not respond immediately. As is his way, he processes the question and carefully prepares an answer.

'Yeah.'

Burunga scratches his head apprehensively.

'Where is he?'

'Down the river.'

'That fucker owes me money. Twenty big ones. Said he was going to pay me and now he's up and left? I've got to send that money home. My daughter needs reading glasses.' With his thumb and forefinger, he rubs his temples, trying to think of a solution. He regains his composure and raises his straw hat to Edgar, bids farewell. He goes with the other companions for their night of entertainment. Edgar Wilson sees he's out of cigarettes. With his arms crossed, chewing on some cloves, he stands there alone, illuminated only by a beam of light from a lamppost.

Milo leaves the slaughterhouse carrying some folders. He greets Edgar, whom he considers to be one of his best employees.

'Aren't you going with the other men, Edgar?'

'I'm waiting for a friend.'

'Say, did you see Zeca today?'

Edgar Wilson shakes his head.

'I haven't seen him in days, and he hasn't even shown up to collect his pay cheque.'

Milo uses a grimy washcloth to wipe the sweat from his neck and forehead. The man has a constant worried look on his face. Edgar Wilson takes pity on his boss for being such a tormented man, veins bulging, his teeth clenched. Sometimes Senhor Milo has trouble breathing and his movements are sluggish.

'I hope that kid didn't get into any trouble,' Milo continues.

'He won't be missed.'

Milo strokes his beard and runs his hand through his hair. He looks suspiciously at Edgar Wilson, who remains unflustered. For now, Milo decides not to ask any more questions and walks towards his truck. He stops along the way and looks back at Edgar:

'The new stun operator arrives tomorrow. I want you to show him around.'

'Yes, sir.'

'His name's Santiago, son of a friend of mine. Came well recommended.'

'Does he have experience in the business, Senhor Milo?'

'He slaughtered reindeer in Finland. Kind of guy who'll kill anything, I think.'

Milo climbs into the truck, starts the engine, turns on the headlights and in a few moments, he pulls away, leaving Edgar Wilson behind with the cows' mooing, and thinking of the reindeer from Christmas movies.

It doesn't take long for the rumble of a backhoe engine to jolt him from the silence. The man driving it has a radio sitting next to him playing disco music. He parks beside Edgar, takes off his cowboy hat, jumps out of the vehicle, leaving the engine running, and shouts:

'Son of a gun! Edgar Wilson, you bastard! I thought you were dead.'

'Vladimir, you old scamp, it's been too long!'

The two embrace and exchange greetings.

'I heard about the coal mine explosion,' says Vladimir.

'I escaped. You'll never see me set foot in a mine again.'

'You really are a son of a bitch, Edgar Wilson. I heard that not even the devil himself could've made it out of a blast like that.'

Edgar's head slumps forward, saddened.

'I dream about that blast every week.' His tone of voice drops and he looks terrified.

Vladimir pats Edgar on the shoulder, shows solidarity and tries to restore the jovial atmosphere from a few seconds before.

Edgar looks at the vehicle.

'My uncle, Piquitito, left it to me as an inheritance. It'll go almost twenty kilometres on a litre of diesel.' With the hem of his shirt sleeve, Vladimir polishes the side of the tractor, bragging about the vehicle like it's a son who's just entered college. His eyes gleam. 'Smokes more than a charcoal pit, but it's all mine. That backhoe's the only thing of value I have in this life.'

Edgar Wilson walks around the vehicle assessing each compartment, and, even in the low light, he can make out the details.

'Last week they offered me seventy thousand for it. I didn't even want to hear it.'

'It really is beautiful.'

Vladimir points to the rear of the tractor, to the most powerful part, the excavator.

'I changed out the whole assembly. The arm, the boom, the bucket, all brand new. Sometimes, I find myself just looking and drooling over those parts.'

Edgar Wilson takes it in, admiring.

'I got a loan from the bank and now I'm paying it back. Working overtime. But thank God there's no shortage of work. Round here, everybody wants to dig a well, a pit, make a hole of some kind.'

Vladimir's name and a phone number are written on the side of the tractor.

'You like it here, Edgar?'

'I've got nothing to complain about. I slaughter cattle and my boss is happy with me. There's no shortage of work.'

'You've always been good at this. Since you were a kid, you could slaughter anything.'

They stand in silence for a few moments. Pensive.

'You still smoke?' asks Vladimir.

'Like a coke furnace.'

Vladimir chuckles and takes a pack of cigarettes from his plaid shirt pocket. Edgar Wilson takes one.

'The work here never ends. Tomorrow another stun operator arrives.'

Vladimir takes a drag on his cigarette and holds the smoke in for a few seconds.

'This is a pretty lucrative business,' he says, choking on the smoke. He catches his breath and continues: 'As long as there's a cow in this world, there'll be a guy willing to kill it.'

'And another one willing to eat it,' Edgar Wilson concludes after a long drag. He exhales the cigarette smoke, releasing not only everything in his lungs, but all the disquiet in his heart. Even the clouds in his thoughts dissipate.

Vladimir drops his cigarette butt on the ground and stamps it out. The front piece, the loader, is lowered, containing a few bags of potatoes, oranges, crates of beer, a Styrofoam cooler, and some leftover cartons. Vladimir stoops over the loader and grabs two cold beer cans from the cooler. He tosses one to Edgar Wilson. They climb onto the tractor and head to the bar in the lightless night, rattling off memories of long-gone days to the sound of disco tunes.

Chapter 3

The river is deserted. It's a dead river, and it's rare to find anyone fishing on it. Some use small, rudimentary boats to cross it on a calm day, and others take a chance on contaminated fish still flopping about. A fish's eyes, even after it's dead, gleam, reflecting the sunlight. A ruminant's eyes are black as night. Inside them is only darkness, and it cannot be trespassed. Perpetually unfathomable.

It's called Rio das Moscas, and ever since slaughter-houses began to spring up around the region known as Ruminant Valley, its clean waters have brimmed with blood. All kinds of things, organic and inorganic, lie at the bottom. Human and animal.

The wind shakes the tree branches and makes the grass lie back on itself, creates ripples on the surface of the river, its waters enveloped in hollow silence between the mountains, which lends a feeling of eternity to the valley's landscape.

The sun is covered by a thin layer of clouds; the sultry heat creates a slight fug, blunted by the occasional gust of wind. Edgar Wilson looks around and up, studying the walls that surround him. The wind blows through the gaps, making its sinuous way into the valley. He takes a deep breath. He breathes in more than air, he breathes in the wind that travels everywhere, the wind that has the privilege of belonging everywhere. It is impossible to know its path, to pursue it or to catch up with it.

Edgar checks the time on his watch. It's still very early. He gets up from the tree trunk where he's been sitting and returns to the pickup truck. He'd stopped there for a few minutes, to feel and breathe in the wind blowing alongside him. Once again, he'd been asked to take an invoice to the hamburger plant, first thing in the morning, before his shift.

Skirting along the banks of the river, its turbid waters reflecting the early morning sun, Edgar Wilson drives at a relaxed pace. As he passes through the gate to the slaughterhouse parking lot, he notices that the wooden sign with the place's name is loose on one side. He thinks about returning later to straighten it. It says 'Touro do Milo Slaughterhouse', with a drawing of a bull's head in brown. But they slaughter everything there: steer, heifers, sheep, hogs, rabbits, buffaloes and bulls. They take anything. As long as someone else pays for it.

Edgar Wilson gives a quick knock on the half-open door to his boss's office. Milo grumbles for him to enter. Without saying a word, Edgar hands him a document, though he doesn't know much about it.

'Edgar, we've got a shipment arriving soon, from far away. They're Lebanese cows. They've travelled for almost a month, and they'll be in bad shape when they get here.'

Milo pauses, checking the document he's just received from Edgar, who, in turn, wonders what Lebanese cows look like and if they require any different handling.

'The good news is Santiago has arrived and starts working with you today. He'll be in the next box over. We're going to streamline the work.' As he says this, Milo raises his hands to the sky. Streamlining must be something like Divine Providence, thinks Edgar Wilson.

'Can I count on you, Edgar?'

'At your service, sir.'

Milo slaps the table. Now he's visibly excited about the Lebanese cows and the reindeer slaughterer.

'One more thing... it's about Zeca. I think you do know where he is.'

Edgar Wilson doesn't give the runaround or deny things. He doesn't lie and he's never known how to. At Mass, he was always told that lying is a thing of the devil.

'I do know, sir.'

Milo waits for the rest of his answer, but Edgar says nothing. Milo asks the question again:

'So, where is he?'

'In the river.'

Milo sits in suspicious silence. He lowers his head slightly and looks at his hands, clasped on top of the desk.

'Rio das Moscas?'

'Yes sir.'

'And how'd he wind up there, Edgar Wilson?' asks Milo with an inquisitive look after raising his head and wiping his face with a washcloth.

'Put him there myself. I knocked him on the head, then threw him in the river.'

'Why did you do that, Edgar?'

'He mistreated the cattle. He was no good.'

'That's a crime, Edgar. You killed a man.'

'No, Senhor Milo. I've killed more than one. Just the men who were no good.'

Milo decides to keep quiet. He knows Edgar Wilson's loyalty, knows his methods, and he knows that Zeca really was useless. No one had reported him missing, and if anybody came looking for the boy, he would simply say that he never showed up for work again. That he doesn't know where he's gone off to. Just as no one questions death in the slaughterhouse, the death of Zeca, whose rational faculties were on par with the ruminants, would surely be ignored. Senhor Milo knows cattlemen, he's cut from the same cloth. No one goes unpunished. They're men of cattle and blood.

The old truck rattles in the distance, moving at no more than fifty kilometres an hour. The ruts in the road are deep in some parts and cause the trailer to careen from side to side. The clouds covering the sun have dissipated. The brightness in the sky ensures that every man in the slaughterhouse is chased by his shadow, a shadow darker than most of the workers there. The truck bed is strapped to the cab with frayed rope, the tyres are bald, and the rusty bumper gives the vehicle a decrepit appearance. The men tumble out of the bed, the older and heavier ones brace themselves against the gate before hitting the ground. A bottle of cachaça has already been consumed during the trip. The smell of booze mixes with bad breath and the odour of the entrails that occasionally fall to the ground and are never completely cleared away.

Each man goes to his post under the watchful eye of the slaughterhouse foreman, Bronco Gil. Tall, with straight hair and tanned skin, and exceptionally strong, he always wears braces and leather boots, even in the heat. He is a self-proclaimed hunter. When a cow breaks free and escapes, he's able to capture it quickly. When a jaguar or wild boar threatens the cattle's safety, he'll sit for days and nights on end in the woods, waiting to ambush it. If a disagreement between the employees oversteps the limits of peaceful coexistence, he knows how to deal with it. Bronco Gil is a mediator, a hunter, a butcher, and one of the vilest individuals Edgar Wilson has ever met.

Despite his ability to handle a shotgun, he prefers a bow and arrow. He is the son of an indigenous woman and a white rancher. Until the age of twelve, he lived with a tribe where outsiders were not allowed, cut off from the world and immersed in a culture not much given to affection. He accidentally lost one of his testicles in an initiation ritual into adulthood. This made him quieter but more aggressive. Some time later, his father decided to go fetch him and take him to live on the ranch, as he needed a helper. In exchange for some tins of potted meat and lard, Bronco Gil was whisked away to a region far removed from the tribe. His father, by then an old man and a widower, had lost his three other sons, who'd spent weeks hunting down two jaguars that had been circling the ranch's cattle. Overnight, the old man found himself alone and with no heirs, so he decided to rescue Bronco Gil and try to civilise him before it was too late. That's the way the old man thought. But instead civilisation barbarised him, and what little affection he'd known became like the dust on the ground he walked upon. Civilised, wearing boots and braces, and combing his hair back with Mutamba and Juá hair tonic, he was taught to hunt for pleasure and to never turn his back on anyone. They lived together, father and son, for ten years, until the old man died of a heart attack while riding among the cornfields.

On his own, Bronco Gil lost the farm, the horses, and two pickup trucks at card tables. The rest of what he had was spent on hookers and booze. Late one night, walking home drunk, propped up by two women, they were run over and left for dead. The deserted stretch of road prevented help from arriving for eight hours. The women didn't make it; he was rescued in time. But his left eye didn't stand a chance. A vulture ate it while his right eye watched. In its place was now one made of glass; brown, like the real one, prone to popping loose from its socket now and again.

Bronco Gil rolls a cigarette and tucks it behind his ear. He'll probably light it at lunchtime. He picks up a clipboard and with a black pen takes attendance. He knows each one by name and nickname. Zeca's name is still on the page, but it hasn't been checked off for several days.

The delivery of Lebanese cows is already running late. Edgar Wilson greets Bronco Gil as he walks past and heads to the locker room, where he will get ready for work. He puts on bloodstained jeans and a threadbare beige T-shirt, black rubber boots and a white jacket. On his head, a faded cap with blood spatters.

In the stun box, he finds Santiago leaning against the wall, waiting for him. He's not very tall, but he's strong. He has a few tattoos on his arms and neck, and his long hair is tied back with a rubber band.

'You must be Edgar Wilson,' says Santiago, reaching out to shake his hand.

Edgar accepts the handshake. Santiago is a restless, anxious type. He darts around and picks his nose constantly.

'I used to slaughter reindeer in Finland.'

'You got any experience with cattle?'

'Yeah, I used to slaughter cattle on a farm in the Irish countryside, until I ended up in Finland with the reindeer.'

Santiago smiles the entire time he talks, a nervous grin. That kind of agitation won't do the cattle any good, thinks Edgar Wilson.

'Over there,' continues Santiago, 'we had to chase down the reindeer. They're trapped inside a pen, and you've got to be real quick, quick as hell, and grab one by the neck, by the leg.' As he speaks, he moves his hands around, hops up and down, twirls from side to side. 'And they have big ol' horns, like this... they're sawed off to make them shorter, but they'll still go right through you if you're not careful, you've got to always be on your toes. They're very fast animals.' The boy's voice is shrill and racing. Edgar Wilson digests the conversation with curiosity. 'And I'm a very fast guy. You grab them and then, boom, you just slit their throats. It's all so fast. Once I see the blood sinking deep into the snow... then I can relax.'

Edgar Wilson is transfixed. His gaze is frozen on the boy. He tries to picture the white snow; he'd never met anybody who'd seen snow. He thinks about blood against the whiteness of the ice. For the first time, he wanted to see snow.

'Here you just need to strike the steer's forehead with a mallet. That's all. And you must be quick. There's no room for error, otherwise the animal suffers.'

Santiago starts hopping from side to side as if warming up to enter a wrestling ring. He stretches his arms out behind him and to the sides. He spreads his legs apart and moves his hips. As Edgar Wilson gives him instructions, he starts getting dressed: a white jumpsuit with a huge zipper down the back, rubber gloves, a rubber cap and ski goggles.

When Edgar completes his instructions, Santiago turns around and asks him to zip up the huge zipper that extends from his buttocks to the nape of his neck. Edgar zips it with one strong tug. Santiago adjusts his ski goggles, securing the elastic band behind his head, and emphatically declares he's ready.

Edgar Wilson realises that those goggles are very effective. It's just what he needs to keep the blood out of his eyes.

'Where'd you find those?' asks Edgar, pointing to the goggles.

'I brought them back from Finland. I used them for skiing. They're ski goggles.'

Edgar Wilson knows he'll never find ski goggles in a place like this, since there's nothing but dirt, dust and mud. Santiago praises the practicality of the goggles as part of his work uniform.

'I can try to get you a pair.'

'How's that?'

'I've got a friend who used to fix sledges in Finland, and he came back the same day as me. He opened up a machine shop with his brothers. It's far away, but I know he had a whole bunch of these goggles. I left some of my things with him, and he's gonna send me everything as soon as he can.'

'You reckon he'd sell me a pair?'

'I'll talk to him, and I'll let you know.'

Edgar Wilson nods in appreciation and goes to the corner of the box, returning with two mallets. One, with a white line on the wooden handle, has his name written on it in blue ink. The other he hands to Santiago, saying 'Follow me.' Edgar positions himself in the box and signals to let the first steer in. The animal is led down a short, narrow chute that leads to the stun box. The more skittish ones get shocked with a stick to make them walk. A window opens and the animal, crammed inside the narrow space, cannot turn around or retreat. Edgar Wilson makes a shushing sound and touches the steer's forehead. It grows less agitated, its eyes less terrified. But the smell of the blood of other ruminants killed in that same place, the smell of death that emanates from Edgar Wilson and his eyes, so full of complacency, tell the animal it will die. Edgar Wilson dips his right thumb into the pot of lime and makes the sign of the cross on the steer's forehead, raises the mallet, and strikes the centre of the cross. One, single, bone-cracking blow, and the animal is out cold on the ground. Immediately, the side wall of the chute is raised, and the steer is pulled out by another employee, who will take it to the bleeding room.

After watching the procedure for a few minutes, Santiago starts work in the neighbouring box, and the pace of productivity on the never-ending line of ruminants to be slaughtered picks up, though it never seems to get any shorter. Edgar Wilson thinks about hamburgers as he works, as he swats away flies and wipes the blood spatter from his face. At the hamburger plant, all that white reflects a peace that doesn't exist, a blinding glare that obscures death. They're all killers, each their own kind, performing their role in the slaughter line.

Chapter 4

Bronco Gil checks the time and notes the delay of almost two hours for the shipment of Lebanese cows. When he spots a trio of trucks coming through the farm gates, he tosses his cigarette on the ground and walks over to greet them, pointing to the loading dock, written in red paint on a peeling wall. He waves to Tonho, one of the cowhands in charge of receiving deliveries.

'You were supposed to be done by now. You're two hours late,' says Bronco Gil.

The truck driver, sweaty and visibly tired, climbs out of the cab. He complains about the bad road and a damaged bridge, which allowed only one vehicle to cross at a time. The driver's assistant, on Bronco Gil's orders, opens the back of the first truck, where the cows are huddled together, looking weak. They're tapdancing in their own faeces and urine. Some have fallen over, passed out; others are in a rage. The space is small for that many head of cattle, and from a distance it's impossible to make out absolutely anything in the darkness. Only the smell and the sound of the mooing verify the vehicle's contents.

A wooden ramp is placed at the back and the cows, their wide eyes brimming with blood and death, exit one-by-one in a frenzy of goading, shouting and kicking. Then they're sent to an open and empty lairage pen that's been prepared for them. There's water in the trough already, and even though they're hungry and have spent the past several days on a strict diet, they won't be able to eat anything.

Bronco Gil goes to the pen and begins to separate the good cattle from the weak. When all the trucks are unloaded, six cows have died. Four remain under observation, due to their frail condition.

The dead cattle are placed, one by one, onto a forklift and dumped at the slaughterhouse's makeshift crematorium, where the furnace is already lit. The smell will attract many dogs over the course of the day. Cremation always takes time.

That's all there is to do with dead cattle, as the animal might be diseased, and the meat contaminated. Even so, little is wasted. The ones under observation will have until the next day to respond to treatment with water, feed, and spray baths, otherwise they'll be thrown into the furnace, too.

Senhor Milo approaches with a tense look on his face, wiping the sweat from his brow. He looks uneasy. He inspects the work being done and assesses the quality of the incoming cattle. He waves Bronco Gil over.

'I got a call saying some Israeli cows got mixed in with this load.' He pauses and looks at the cattle. He knits his brows, as if by pulling a face things might become clearer. He lowers his voice and, embarrassed, confesses: 'I can't tell the difference. Do you see anything?'

Bronco Gil looks closely at the cattle. He walks over to some cows that are hurrying toward the pen, touches one of them, sniffs it, studies its teeth, its tail, and stares into its unfathomable eyes. He turns to the boss and, looking slightly bashful, replies:

'No, sir. These Lebanese cows are very similar to ours.' Milo scratches his head.

'The person in charge of the shipment asked us to separate the Lebanese cows from the Israeli cows, because all the meat is going to a packing plant that supplies directly to an entire neighbourhood full of Lebanese folks. And they can tell the difference by how the meat tastes.'

'How do they do that?' asks Bronco Gil.

'It's got something to do with the grass that grows in Lebanese soil, and the water they drink. They said the Israeli cows broke through the fence and were grazing illegally on the Lebanese pasture, and the cowhands ended up mixing them all up when they loaded the trucks.'

'But if they were grazing on Lebanese land, then surely the meat all tastes the same.'

'I thought the same thing... they must do it all the time.'

'Nobody will be able to tell the difference.'

Milo still looks unsure. His concern is moving, and he fears inciting a war between two enemy countries. He orders one of the cowhands to call Edgar Wilson, who is in the stun box.

'Yes, Senhor Milo. You wanted to see me?' says Edgar, wiping his bloodied hands, oblivious to the blood spatter on his face.

'Edgar, we've got a big problem.'

Edgar Wilson nods obligingly.

'There's a problem with this shipment of Lebanese cows.' Milo takes a breath before continuing. 'Some Israeli cows got mixed in with the Lebanese cows, and those cows are enemies. We need to know which is which.' Milo awaits a reaction from Edgar Wilson, who stands motionless, waiting for more details. 'The Lebanese and the Israelis are enemies,' the boss continues. 'They won't eat each other's cows. And these cows are going to a packing plant that only sells to Lebanese. Do you see the problem we've got on our hands?'

Edgar nods slightly.

'Am I going to slaughter these cows?'

'They'll send a Muslim to do it,' replies Milo. 'It's their tradition. They have to call upon God at the time of slaughter. They have special men for that.'

Edgar Wilson doesn't respond, but he thinks about how it sounds a lot like what he does when he slaughters one of these animals.

'You're very good with cattle and I want to know if you can tell who's who.'

'I couldn't tell any difference,' says Bronco Gil.

'How'd they get mixed up?' asks Edgar Wilson.

'Israeli cows like to graze on Lebanese territory,' explains Bronco Gil.

'They need to build a taller fence,' says Edgar Wilson. 'That way the cows won't go from one side to the other.'

'I agree with you, Edgar. That must be the problem, the size of the fence. If those bastards had a big enough fence, I wouldn't be here now, shitting myself, afraid of putting Israeli cows on Lebanese plates.' Senhor Milo is so upset he's short of breath. 'I don't want them to come over here and bomb my slaughterhouse... I don't want any trouble with these folks. They're assassins. They kill all the time.'

'I can take a look, if that's okay.'

'Please do, right away.'

Edgar Wilson enters the slaughterhouse and returns with a tin of yellow paint. Head down, he goes to the lairage pen where all the cows are gathered, still agitated. He walks among them and observes them, one by one. Santiago would have to handle slaughtering the cattle on his own for the next hour.

At first, it was impossible to make out anything, not even local cows from foreign cows, but he's sure at least one detail will catch his attention. He shushes as he treads gently on the ground, letting himself become part of the herd. He sees three cows backed into a corner, their faces right up together, as if they were plotting with each other. A fourth cow draws near and adopts a similar position to the other three. Edgar Wilson approaches and claps his hands, attempting to disperse the group, but the quartet remains unfazed. He fetches other cows for the quartet to socialise with. He finds the cattle's selectiveness odd. The rest of the cows moo loudly and refuse to approach the others.

For a few moments, Edgar Wilson yields to the late afternoon sun that has not yet fully set, but that is rushing headlong into a moonless, starless night. He knows how to listen in silence, even when others are just sighing or snorting. Life in the country has made him like the ruminants, and being a cattleman, he is able to strike a perfect balance between the fears of irrational beings and the abominable reverie of those who dominate them. He sinks two fingers into the paint can and marks the foreheads of the four cornered cows.

'Get a load of that, he did it,' Bronco Gil says to the boss, who just grins.

Edgar Wilson steps outside the pen and ambles towards them. Along the way, he lights a cigarette. The smell of beef crackling in the crematorium begins to attract the dogs.

'The ones marked in yellow, sir.'

'Good job, Edgar Wilson,' says Senhor Milo, feeling both proud and relieved.

Edgar pushes the slaughterhouse door open, but before he goes inside, he looks at the tall trail of smoke issuing from behind the stable. It dissipates in the wind before it touches the clouds.

He walks through the door and gets back to work, for the line is long and the work, never ending.

Chapter 5

Bronco Gil finishes checking the cattle in one of the lairage pens and orders one of the cowhands to take them for bathing, which is done in a stable with sprinklers installed on the ceiling. Then, as a group, the animals are sprayed down with warm water, cleaned before the kill.

At his feet is a miscarried calf, covered in maggots, part-eaten and swathed in a dark film from the dried-up placenta. This is the second time in three days. He grabs a shovel, scoops it up off the ground, and leaves it at the crematorium.

'Again?' asks the cowhand in charge of cremating cattle.

'I just don't get it,' says Bronco Gil, filled with worry. 'This hardly ever happens.'

'They must be sick.'

'Maybe, but I don't think it's disease. The heifers are pretty healthy, even.'

Bronco Gil is silent for a few moments, until he is interrupted by the cowhand.

'It's been a while since a calf was born around here.'

Bronco Gil looks at the dead calf, now sprawled on a

cart. He tries to remember how long it's been since he's seen new calves in the pasture.

'At least six months,' mumbles Bronco Gil.

'Something like that,' says the man, dragging the calf to the furnace with the help of another cowhand. He takes a breath and continues, 'I've cremated a lot of miscarriages over the last few months.'

Tonho waves to Bronco Gil, who, as he leaves the crematorium, notices a small group of people coming through the gate. These are the poor souls who live nearby and survive off the cattle that die in transit. Whenever a shipment arrives, they come through the gate soon after. There's always someone out on the roads on guard duty, watching the trucks come in.

Bronco Gil can't stand these people, but deep down he feels sorry for them. He walks over to intercept them before they get too close to the truck still parked in the yard.

'There's nothing here for you today.'

'Mister, we saw the truck pull in,' says one of the women in the group. She wears a printed scarf tied around her head; her black skin is dry like tanned leather and her lips are swollen.

'But there's nothing for you today,' insists Bronco Gil.

'Don't you have any dead ones?' asks an old hunch-backed woman, wrapped in a yellow shawl.

'We've already sent them to the crematorium. Get on out of here. The boss doesn't like you hanging around.'

'For the love of God, sir. The children are so hungry. And our crops aren't yielding,' pleads one of the women.

'It's true, Mister, there's nothing in the house,' adds a mixed-race girl with blonde hair and freckled cheeks.

Bronco Gil looks around. He takes another cigarette from behind his ear and lights it. It's always miserable having to deal with this. With the hunger, with the women and children. It's a hell few people know. The hell he has to deal with is under the sun, full of hunger and dust.

He sighs. He gazes out into the distance.

'Stay outside, past the gate. Hide in the brush because my boss doesn't want you all around here. And if I lose my job, I swear I'll kill every last one of you. I'll kill you, and skin you all, you hear?'

They nod along.

'I'll send a man over with a piece of the dead steer. And if anybody gets sick from the meat, don't even think about coming back here to complain. You already know what'll happen.'

'God bless you, Mister. May God bless you twofold,' says the old woman, reaching for Bronco Gil's hand.

'Now get on out of here.'

With that, they hurry out the slaughterhouse gates and Bronco Gil goes back to work. He orders Tonho to cut off a few parts from one of the dead cows and take it to the women on the other side of the gate. Nearly an hour later, Tonho dumps a sack of fat pieces of cow at the women's feet, who have to contend with the pack of hungry dogs that circle the slaughterhouse whenever the crematorium furnace is lit. They thank him and head back down the dry, rough road full of rabid dogs.

Once again, Burunga has his head submerged inside a barrel of water and is surrounded by men anxiously awaiting the result of the stopwatch old Emetério insists on holding. When he emerges, he's set another record and collects the coins in his straw hat, right after he hikes up his trousers. Burunga is in urgent need of money, he needs to get some glasses for his daughter. He hopes he's got enough breath in him to make it.

The lunch break is almost over, and Edgar Wilson leaves the canteen to enjoy his last few minutes of rest sitting on a tree stump, protected by the shade of a guava tree.

Santiago walks over, tying back his hair with a rubber band. He takes a piece of gum from his pocket and pops it into his mouth. He sits down on an overturned paint can beside Edgar Wilson.

'It really is tough work,' he says, getting no reaction from Edgar Wilson, who watches the cows in the pasture. 'I sure missed this heat. Sometimes I wouldn't see the sun for months. It was just cold and ice, and this blinding whiteness, you couldn't see a thing.'

'What's snow like?' asks Edgar Wilson.

'It's not like anything we have around here. It's so pretty.'

'Do they have hogs over there?'

'I didn't see any hogs. But there were moose. I slaughtered moose too when they paid me to. I even brought back some tinned moose meat, I used to eat it all the time.'

'What's it taste like?'

'Like smoked meat. I still have some if you want to try it.'

Edgar nods his head in thanks. He goes back to watching the cows grazing.

'What is it you're always looking at in this pasture?' Santiago asks uneasily, rising to his feet.

'The cows... they're different.'

Santiago looks out over the pasture but sees nothing he would deem out of the ordinary.

'Did you notice that?' Edgar Wilson is pointing at something. Santiago squints his eyes and raises his chin in curiosity. 'Some of the cows are facing west instead of north. That's no good.'

'But why, Edgar? What does it matter which way they graze?'

'They only graze to the north, and some of them have been facing west for days.'

'And what does that mean?'

'That there's something very wrong going on.'

'What do you think it is?'

'I don't know... I've never seen this happen... they've lost their way. That's no good.'

The north wind blows hard between the mountains and carries with it the scent of ripe pomegranates. The last traces of daylight had faded a few minutes earlier, the sunset's trail obscured by the grey of early evening.

When night falls, the residents of Ruminant Valley tend to shut their doors and windows tight. They believe that everything that seems improbable during the day can overcome the darkness. It's when thoughts that were once impossible become possible; when hushed whispers swell, and above all, when that layer of darkness cloaks anything suspicious. The figures, the voids, long shadows, all of it brought on by the night, which is immense, and its reaches infinite.

During the day, the dividing line of the horizon, its boundaries, can be clearly distinguished. That's how it is, looking at the river. At night, however, none of those lines are discernible. Only darkness connects water and sky. The horizon, that faint division visible in the light of day, doesn't exist at night. At night, when the body is resting, there's a better sense of what is going on inside. Reflections, with no dividing lines or borders.

The men who don't live in the slaughterhouse dormitory have already left to go home. Only those separated from the cattle by a partition are left. Night has just fallen, but there will be no fun today. Most will go to sleep after their supper. Milo is still in his office, mashing calculator buttons with his fingertips.

Edgar Wilson and Bronco Gil sit side by side on the same tree stump under the guava tree, sharing a bottle of beer. Edgar tends to hang around there whenever he can, watching the pasture, which is silent, as it should be, when night comes.

'Moose meat? I tell you what, I've never seen one of those in all my days hunting.'

'He said he still has a few tins. Said he used to slaughter moose, too.'

'Guess he finds work wherever he goes.'

'Moose look like deer.'

'Oh, right... I've hunted lots of deer. They're fast.'

The low mooing that reverberates around the farm sounds like the lapping of calm waters. The valley is a place filled with trees, undergrowth, small streams, waterfalls, and it blooms a reddish hue due to the roses and pomegranates, but mostly because of the blood. It's impossible to tell from a distance, or even smell it, but the roses that bloom along Rio das Moscas have gotten darker over the years, feeding on the river's bloody waters.

The next day, a group of university students will visit the slaughterhouse and then head to the hamburger plant to see the entire journey made by meat. Milo initially rejected the idea, but he acquiesced after pleas from the professor who will accompany the students. They don't know what they're in for, Edgar Wilson thinks. Maybe they won't watch the whole process. For sure no one leaves a slaughterhouse unscathed. The first time he slaughtered a cow, Edgar felt the rush of the animal's blood and heard the crack of its skull. In the ruminant's eyes, ever unfathomable, all mist and darkness dissipated. He witnessed his own image before him, reflected in the eyes of the cow, moments before its death. The image of the beast. Every day it's him he sees when he kills, because he's learned to see under the fog that shrouds the animal's eyes.

The beer is almost gone, and Bronco Gil, quieted, nods off with his head hanging forward. Edgar Wilson hears a snort coming from the pasture. Hooves hit the ground, echoing to the outer reaches of the farm. One long, gruff moo, followed by the trot of a cow, which moves forward and crashes into the fence. Bronco Gil raises his head and opens his eyes. The cow is slamming itself against the fence, trying to break it. It cuts itself on the barbed wire.

'Sweet Lord in heaven, what the hell is going on?' Bronco Gil exclaims, taking off his hat.

Edgar Wilson gets up but doesn't move. Bronco Gil, now standing, steps back gently. The fence sways and the posts driven into the ground begin to pull loose. The barbed wire stretches but does not break.

'She's being attacked,' says Bronco Gil, reaching for the revolver inside the holster strapped around his ribs.

'No, she isn't,' says Edgar Wilson.

Bronco Gil fires a shot into the air to try to scare off the supposed predator. With only one eye and the darkness, he's not sure what he sees. Edgar Wilson, his gaze fixed on the pasture, watches every movement and declares there to be no predators.

The cow becomes more aggressive and starts to ram one of the posts, which snaps, dropping the fence low enough to be able to jump over. In a rage, it sprints around the farm, then stops for a moment and thumps its front hoof against the dirt. It sniffs for something. Bronco Gil still fears a predator is nearby, probably a jaguar or a wild boar. But the remaining cattle in the pasture are huddled in a corner, just lowing.

The cow turns from side to side as if looking for guidance. It seems to be settling down. Bronco Gil motions for Edgar Wilson to follow him, grabs the rope he keeps attached to his belt, and makes a lasso to capture it. The two of them tread slowly and deliberately, beating a path round some trees so they can take the cow by surprise, but first they'll need to position themselves in the animal's blind spot. Bronco Gil jerks the lasso around the cow and loses his glass eye, which slips from the socket and falls to the ground.

'My eye fell out,' he yells, down on the ground, digging through the weeds. 'My goddamn eye fell out!'

The cow begins a desperate race towards the slaughterhouse, letting out one long, defiant-sounding moo, and throws itself headfirst against the wall with such force that its body lifts off the ground, then falls, writhing until it stops mooing.

Edgar Wilson approaches the animal, one hoof still shuddering. Its eyes are wide, petrified. He reaches down and gently touches its fractured forehead, making the sign of the cross. He does not find his reflection in the cow's eyes. This time, he was not there.

Not even the moon can separate heaven from earth. It's as if that vastness had swallowed up the valley, as if Edgar Wilson were inside the belly of God, at the beginning of creation, when everything was darkness.

Chapter 6

Bronco Gil watches the pasture. His shadow lengthens until it touches the partially destroyed fence. The day is hot and dusty. Beneath the sun, the men are all already hard at work, relentlessly pursued by their own shadows. As he walks, Bronco Gil's shadow invades the pasture and blankets part of a dozy cow chewing on a handful of grass. He bends down and fills his cupped hand with earth. He sniffs it, then tosses it aside. Standing back up, he searches the barbed wire fence for some sign of the animal that attacked the cow. Not only does he not find a single hair, but he also sees that the fence has no damage, apart from what the cow itself did. He shoos away some cows that are huddling nearby and searches for tracks from a jaguar or a wild boar. He finds nothing.

He is determined to stay up all night and keep watch. Because of the panic he witnessed last night, he imagines it will be a difficult animal to catch. He devises a few strategic traps and considers the predator's entry and escape routes.

Crouched down, sniffing at another handful of earth, Edgar Wilson's shadow falls over him.

'What do you want?'

'The students just arrived.' Bronco Gil rises to his feet. He wears a shotgun slung across his back. His face expresses dismay. He looks out over the meadow that spreads as far as his eye can see, but he knows that the horizon is expansive, and its limits are not visible from this point.

'I've got to find that bastard,' says Bronco Gil. 'I don't understand how it got in. There's no trace. The fence is fine here and here,' he says, pointing in several directions, as disoriented as the cow before it died, as distressed as an animal in the line for slaughter.

'There were no predators here,' says Edgar Wilson.

'Then how do you explain that?' asks Bronco Gil, getting worked up again.

Edgar Wilson is silent for some time. He just looks out at the grass lying flat in the breeze, and the bright, sunny day.

'I'm going to find this animal and I'm going to need help.'

'You can count on me.'

'It may be that tonight they'll come in packs.' Bronco Gil adjusts his hat. 'So, let's gather the most ruthless men in this place. Do you know how to use one of these?' he asks, showing his shotgun.

Edgar Wilson nods.

'Great. I prefer my bow and arrow. Don't wear yourself out, we have a lot of work to do tonight.'

Bronco Gil leaves the pasture and goes to meet the students, who are eager to see the production line. The group is made up of eleven students and their teacher.

'Hi, I'm Professor Aristeu. These are my students. Thank you for having us at such an... interesting place.' The man is as jumpy as a wild bullock and, speaking with a permanent grin on his face, nods his head in agreement with whatever is said. 'We are so excited to get a taste of

46

the workers' day-to-day lives and visit the cattle facilities and learn how...' He chuckles. 'Well, learn how the meat makes it onto our plates every day. From here we'll go to the hamburger plant that processes your meat.' He stops short and slaps his forehead, as if to say, how foolish of me. 'I mean, the meat you produce here.'

Bronco Gil is silent the whole time. When the man finishes speaking, he shouts for Tonho and asks him to take them to the pen of cattle already picked for slaughter.

'I would like to thank Senhor Milo for his kindness, for allowing us to visit such a... curious place,' says the professor.

'I'll make sure he gets the message. Now, if you gentlemen and ladies will excuse me.' Bronco Gil raises his hat, showing that he also has good manners, and leaves.

Edgar Wilson raises the mallet and strikes the first steer of the second batch of the day. Santiago has been doing a good job and maintains his frenetic pace, doing warmups and stretches before entering the box. Edgar Wilson is satisfied with his new colleague's work and realises how right he was to have dumped Zeca at the bottom of the river. So far no one has come looking for him. In those places where blood mixes with soil and water, it's difficult to make any sort of distinction between man and animal. Edgar feels so attuned with the ruminants, with their unfathomable eyes and the pulse of blood coursing through their veins, that his mind sometimes goes astray and questions who is man, and who is ruminant.

A pair of eyes, pupils dilated behind thick glasses, watches him work through a crack in the box's wooden wall. He turns his attention back to his work and realises he's face-to-face with the cow with a brown teardrop on its forehead. He makes the mark of the cross with lime and, after seeing himself reflected in its eyes, he raises the mallet and strikes. A trickle of blood squirts across his face and splatters in his right eye. He wipes his face with the hem of his shirt and asks the worker not to release the next one, as he needs to go wash out his eye.

Santiago realises what happened and tells Edgar Wilson that he got him a pair of ski goggles, and they were already on their way, sent with a batch of his personal belongings that were with his friend from Finland. My days with blood in my eyes are numbered, Edgar thinks.

When he exits the bathroom, he runs into the group of students, walking in a line through the corridors of the slaughterhouse, looking like distressed cattle on their way to be stunned. Most are having difficulty breathing, so they hold a handkerchief over their nose and mouth. Some have decided to step back as they move toward the bloodletting area, from the mere thought of what they were about to see. Standing in front of those steers and heifers shackled upside down by their hind legs, their throats slit, gushing litres of blood into fetid vats, mixed with vomit and excrement, wasn't exactly what they had in mind. Nobody will get out of here unscathed. This thought makes Edgar Wilson glad. He quickens his pace as he strides towards the stun box, when Tonho calls him over to introduce him to the class.

'He's the one who puts the cattle to sleep.'

Everyone turns to him. Professor Aristeu, clutching a gingham handkerchief over his nose, approaches, and reaches out to shake his hand.

'How do you do? I'm Professor Aristeu.'

'Edgar Wilson.'

'So, Edgar Wilson, tell us a little about your work,' he says excitedly, his voice muffled under the handkerchief.

'I'm the stun operator.'

Professor Aristeu is impressed by the man before him. 'Oh, right, fascinating. We just saw the stunning process through a crack in the wall. It's hard work. Must take a lot of physical strength, a lot of concentration. Not all the students wanted to look.' Professor Aristeu is interrupted by the voice of one of his students.

'What's it like killing cattle all day long? Don't you think this is murder? Don't you think that slaughtering these animals is a crime?'

Edgar turns toward the voice and comes face-to-face with that pair of eyes with dilated pupils, protected by thick, red-rimmed glasses. The young woman, dressed in a long skirt and a white button-down blouse, constantly makes notes in a black notebook. Edgar looks at her two-tone, black and brown leather shoes. They have a silver buckle on the side. They're delicate and clean. He thinks of Burunga's daughter, who needs glasses for her bad eyes.

'I do.'

Everyone is silent, perhaps waiting for him to finish his answer, perhaps surprised by its brevity. The woman stammers as she attempts one more question, but this time her voice is more reticent and fragile:

'So, do you consider yourself a murderer?'

'I do.'

The short answer silences the woman and ensures the others stay quiet. Professor Aristeu smiles, pulling the handkerchief away from his nose, and tries to change the subject.

'How long have you worked in this role, Edgar?'

'A couple of years.'

'Oh, right, how wonderful. You must have acquired a lot of experience,' he says, still grinning and swatting away the flies that swarm everywhere.

'Aren't you ashamed?' the woman speaks out again, this time more incisively.

Edgar looks at her. He looks at everyone around him.

He breathes in the scent of the slaughterhouse and fills his lungs. He takes off his cap and combs his hair with his fingers. A few flies land on his short, greasy hair.

'Miss.'

He pauses. Edgar Wilson knows his place and understands his obligations well. He's never been asked about his duties. He deals with cattlemen and destitute women all the time. He is used to the heat, the dust, the flies, the blood, and death. That is what a slaughterhouse is all about. Killing. He had no intention of going across town to question the way they prepare steaks he will never eat. He doesn't care about that. He doesn't care who eats the cows he slaughters; he cares about ordaining the souls of each ruminant that crosses his path. He believes these animals have a soul, and that he must tend to each one when they die. One soul out of five hundred.

'Have you ever eaten a hamburger?'

The woman nods.

'And how do you think it got there?'

The students all exchange glances. Professor Aristeu grins nervously and tries to utter a few words, but Edgar Wilson pushes him aside and heads straight to the woman at the back of the group. She cowers. The others back away. Edgar stares at the woman, waiting for an answer. She lowers her head. Edgar picks up a mallet lying on the ground. It's not his, but it serves his purpose. He hands the mallet to the woman. She doesn't understand. She looks at him, disoriented. He insists and she takes it. He opens the door to the stun box and tells her to enter.

'You can find out if you like. From the very beginning. Get to know the whole process, isn't that what you all came for? If you want to learn how to make your own hamburgers, the process starts here.'

The woman drops the mallet to the ground and starts to cry. A young man who's had a terrified look on his face the whole time, now confronted with the blood on the stun box floor and the putrid smell, bends over and vomits onto Edgar Wilson's rubber boots. Edgar glances at the vomit and ignores it altogether. He puts his cap on, excuses himself, and enters the box, closing the door behind him, without saying another word.

Chapter 7

Old Emetério scoops up the manure inside one of the empty pens with a shovel. He fills buckets with excrement and dumps them into a drum. He took up this new post a few days ago, when he had an accident with a knife he was handling in the rendering room. He's grateful he didn't get fired, or that he didn't cut off his finger. His eyesight is no longer what it used to be, and his hands get stiff every day. His joints are rusty and painful, but the old man won't let anything bring him down. He's still ticking, with a wrinkly smile and straight back.

When he finishes filling a drum of manure, he rolls it to the storage location, where it will sit drying. In a few days it will be sold to a company that makes fertilizer, which sends a truck once a week to fetch large batches of organic matter.

On entering the storage shed, the old man finds Santiago bent over one of the containers.

'What are you doing in here?' asks the old man.

'I just came to pick some mushrooms,' Santiago replies, plucking a few white caps with his fingers.

'Again? That stuff's no good, kid,' he says in his low, raspy voice.

Santiago returns his attention to the drum and continues picking the mushrooms he finds.

'That stuff will drive you crazy,' insists the old man. 'Now scram.'

'I just need a few more, old-timer. I'm almost done.'

Santiago holds a handful of white mushrooms against his chest and leaves the shed, excited.

'Bastard,' Emetério grumbles to himself.

Santiago keeps the mushrooms wrapped inside a piece of cloth in his cupboard. He plans on cooking them later. He pulls out a cardboard box and checks his belongings one more time. Everything is in order, and he takes the ski goggles from the bottom of the box. He checks the elastic band and the frames. They're perfect. He locks the cupboard with a padlock, exits the dormitory and heads towards the stun box.

He straightens his cap and pulls the goggles over his eyes. He enters the box and, as soon as he sees Edgar Wilson, he whistles at him and holds up the goggles. Edgar rests his mallet on the ground. Santiago tosses the goggles to him.

'Give 'em a try!' says Santiago, smiling.

Edgar Wilson grabs the goggles in mid-air and immediately slips the elastic band over his head. He fits them over his nose and looks around. He gives a thumbs up and closed-mouth smile.

'Not a drop of blood in your eyes,' Santiago says, warming up before motioning for the next in line to enter the box.

'Never again,' says Edgar Wilson, as his mallet strikes a cow's forehead.

***

When the last man climbs into the back of the truck, the driver steps gently on the accelerator, and creeps toward the slaughterhouse gates. It's half an hour before nightfall and the only ones around are the cleaners, who prepare the facility for the next day. No matter how hard they scrub, the place is always filthy and stinking. Edgar Wilson comes out of the shower and pulls on some jeans and a black T-shirt. He slips on his only pair of short leather boots, which have better grip and good flexibility. Hunkering down in the brush demands a certain care. He puts on a black hat, an imitation Australian bush hat, and adjusts the cord under his chin.

He goes to sit in his usual spot and starts to peel a guava with a pocketknife. He watches Milo leave early. Every Saturday he meets friends at the bar to play cards and drink. It's his only moment of fun. Sunday is the day of rest, for both the men and the cattle. They never shed blood on Sunday. It is a holy day, according to Milo and the life-long teachings of his Catholic upbringing. Milo usually goes to Mass with his family first thing in the morning, even though he's been drinking, playing cards, and bedding prostitutes the night before. But he considers himself a good man and has never been confronted for his actions. He believes that the sacramental host cleanses him of all impurity and redeems him of all imperfection. And so, by eating Christ's flesh and drinking His blood, he feels part of Christ. But it never occurred to him that by eating the flesh of those cattle and drinking their blood, he would also become part of the animals he slaughters every day. Every Monday Milo goes to work feeling like a man of God: *by the sweat of your brow, you shall eat bread*.

With the tip of his knife, Edgar Wilson removes an insect from the guava. He picks another guava from the tree and, when he slices it in half, he sees it's crawling with bugs. He tosses it aside and sits down again, immersed in his own habitual stillness. Looking out at the pasture ahead, his eyes transfixed, he muses on inscrutable thoughts, as unfathomable as the eyes of ruminants.

Helmuth lounges by the pasture fence, watching the sun set and swatting away the mosquitoes that multiply at that hour, as well as the cicadas, singing their shrill song. He takes the rosary he wears against his chest and says a prayer, his lips in constant motion, occasionally making a hissing noise that mingles with the buzz of the mosquitoes and the cicadas' song. Edgar Wilson wonders what a man like Helmuth asks for in his prayers; maybe the same as him, maybe what every man there asks for.

Santiago comes out of the dormitory holding a tin mug, sipping from time to time, in rhythm with his stride. He goes for a walk around the farm, alone with his headphones. He bumps into Bronco Gil but doesn't seem to notice. He snaps his fingers and wiggles his shoulders. Bronco Gil is carrying a small arsenal and, when he gets to where Edgar Wilson is sitting, throws everything on the ground. Helmuth makes the sign of the cross, tucks the rosary inside his shirt, and approaches the other men.

'I brought a few things. I set some traps at strategic points,' says Bronco Gil. 'We'll get it.'

Helmuth picks out what he wants to use. He takes one of the two shotguns and tries the aim without firing.

'I'll take this one.'

'The safety sticks a little,' says Bronco Gil.

Holding the unloaded weapon, Helmuth tries to figure out the best way to address the defect.

'Edgar, you take the other one,' orders Bronco Gil.

Edgar Wilson takes the shotgun from the ground and opens the barrel, checking that it is unloaded. He stuffs some ammo in his pocket.

The roar of the engine of Vladimir's backhoe silences the mosquitoes and drowns out the cicadas. He parks the vehicle at the loading bay. He gets down holding a rifle and carries a bag of ammunition slung across his back. He's in no hurry, smoking a cigarette he rolled a few hours ago. He greets everyone and complains about some indigestion that's been burning him up inside for the last day.

Night finally settles over their heads. They retreat to a knoll where they set up an observation deck, propped against a felled tree trunk. According to Bronco Gil's calculations, the predator has three possible points of entry to the pastures, and from where they are, they'll be able to identify it as soon as it turns up. Vladimir uses the scope of his rifle to watch from a distance, and the other three take turns with two sets of binoculars. Bronco Gil sharpens the tip of an arrow with a piece of pumice stone, feeling it in the dark. They have to sit in the dark and speak softly, the full moon and starry sky to guide them. An hour of silence and surveillance later, Edgar Wilson takes the bag with the thermos and pours himself some coffee. The others join him. Vladimir gets up and goes to take a leak at the foot of a tree.

'I hope this critter won't take long to show its face,' says Helmuth.

'Was it a jaguar or a wild boar?' asks Vladimir, returning to the group and settling down on the ground.

'I couldn't quite make it out,' says Bronco Gil.

The men burst out laughing. Bronco Gil gets serious.

'Edgar said your eye fell out,' says Vladimir mockingly.

'But my good eye was wide open,' replies Bronco Gil, enraged. He gets up and walks away.

'That Indian son of a bitch...' murmurs Vladimir.

'What about you, Edgar, didn't you see anything?' asks Helmuth.

'There was no predator,' he replies tersely.

'Of course there was,' shouts Bronco Gil, pissing on a tree.

'But you didn't see it,' Helmuth says to Bronco Gil.

'So, Edgar, what did you see?' Vladimir demands.

'The cow threw herself against the side of the slaughterhouse,' Edgar Wilson replies.

'Just like that, out of the blue?' says Vladimir.

'Edgar, you don't know what you're talking about,' says Bronco Gil when he returns.

'I know what I saw. And there were no predators there. Not in the pasture nor outside. The cow killed itself,' concludes Edgar Wilson.

'I once had a horse that refused to eat and it just wasted away until it died,' says Helmuth. 'Couldn't even get it to drink water. Would overturn the trough.'

Bronco Gil asks for silence and the men position themselves.

'I heard something,' he says.

They watch from a distance, searching for any movement in the pastures or the surroundings. There's nothing. After a few moments of silence, Helmuth asks:

'Is that truckload of sheep coming on Monday?'

Edgar Wilson says yes and adds that he doesn't like to slaughter sheep.

'They kneel down and weep when they're about to die,' explains Edgar.

'But the meat's tasty,' remarks Bronco Gil.

'True,' agrees Helmuth.

'One time, back when I was still living in the jungle, we had to capture some wild boar,' Bronco Gil begins. 'The way we did it was we put out some sheep to attract them. The boars ripped them in half and divvied up the pieces. Every day they'd come back in greater numbers, and all the while we were putting up fences. And they always came back in greater numbers. They thought they were hunting the sheep, but by the fifth day they were completely surrounded, and when we drove in the last fence post, we preyed on more than thirty boar. Five sheep for more than thirty boar...'

'Pretty good deal,' Vladimir assesses.

'We put them all in a pen,' Bronco Gil says with delight, 'and we slaughtered them, one by one.'

'Food is what attracts animals and makes them nice and tame,' says Edgar Wilson.

'For that very reason, Edgar. How could that cow go nuts just like that? They're locked up in there, eating and drinking... just waiting to die,' says Vladimir.

'But they don't know that,' replies Helmuth.

'How can you be sure they don't?' asks Edgar Wilson.

They are silent until a noise from the pastures is heard again. Bronco Gil, crouching with the binoculars, says there are strange movements in one of the pastures.

'Now you'll see, Edgar Wilson, if there's a predator or not.'

Propped against the tree trunk, Helmuth eggs them on, saying there might be more than one. The noise in the pasture grows louder.

'Be careful not to shoot any cattle,' says Vladimir.

'Wait,' says Helmuth, beckoning Bronco Gil to lower his bow and arrow. 'It's the dog. It's lil' Uggo walking among the cows.'

'Are you sure?' asks Bronco Gil.

'I'd know that damn mutt anywhere. Yeah, it's him... that's Uggo. He likes to wander around the pastures.'

Disappointed, Bronco Gil lowers his bow:

'I'm going to take a look around, see if I can sniff something out.' And he walks away.

The sun is almost up. Vladimir is dozing, Helmuth and Edgar Wilson are visibly tired. Bronco Gil spent the entire morning sitting in a tree, five metres up, trying to expand his field of view.

There's a commotion in one of the pastures, followed by Uggo barking. They all stand at the ready. Bronco Gil jumps down from the tree and goes to the edge of the knoll. The others look through the binoculars and confirm there is something going on in the pasture. Bronco Gil perks up. He takes a deep breath.

'It's got horns,' says Vladimir, looking through his rifle scope. 'And it's moving real quick.'

The cows grow uneasy, and some grunts now mix with the mooing.

'What kind of goddamn animal is that!' exclaims Helmuth, his eyes glued to his binoculars.

'That's no jaguar,' says Vladimir.

'Or a wild boar,' adds Bronco Gil.

The cows sprint back and forth, crashing into one another. A slight wave of dread overtakes the men, who are unable to identify the animal either by its appearance or by its grunts. A few more minutes and the sun will catch up with them, bringing perfect visibility, but the mounting distress in the pasture leads them downhill, guns at the ready, and they surround the area. The animal races past, defying the men's comprehension because of the way it moves. They have never seen horns so tall or movements so swift. Bronco Gil, with his bow drawn, waits for a clearing to form among the cattle and, when he finds one, he shoots.

The cows are still restless, but nothing else is moving from side to side.

'Did you get it?' shouts Helmuth.

'I think so,' answers Bronco Gil.

'I don't see anything moving,' says Vladimir.

'There's something lying in the middle of the pasture,' says Edgar Wilson as the cows open a large clearing around the fallen animal, still moving slowly.

'It's still alive,' says Edgar Wilson, jumping over the pasture fence and walking quickly to the animal, his shotgun raised.

'I told you, Edgar, I told you there was a predator,' boasts Bronco Gil.

Edgar Wilson touches the animal. The others come up behind him.

'What is it?' asks Vladimir, flustered.

'It's Santiago, the new stun operator. He thinks he's a reindeer.'

Edgar removes the bough of branches strapped to the boy's head with rubber bands and pulls back the jaguar pelt he's wearing.

'What the hell...' babbles Bronco Gil, dumbfounded.

'That's the jaguar hide that hangs in Senhor Milo's office,' says Helmuth.

The arrow had pierced Santiago's shoulder and he moans softly.

'I almost shot him,' says Vladimir.

Edgar Wilson slaps Santiago on the face to wake him up. He opens his eyes. He's very frightened.

'Take him inside,' orders Bronco Gil, and the other men carry him carefully to the kitchen.

Old Emetério is already up, making coffee. He asks what happened. The men explain.

'I warned him about drinking that damn cow-dung mushroom tea. Said it was gonna drive him crazy. I told him.'

After placing Santiago on the long, narrow table, the old man gives him a strong cup of coffee to regain his senses.

'Give him a little nip, old man,' says Bronco Gil.

The old man takes the bottle he keeps stored under his straw tick mattress and yanks out the cork. Edgar

Wilson lifts Santiago's head and old Emetério pours the cachaça down his throat.

'Bastard!' he exclaims as Santiago spits the drink in his face.

'Hold him,' Bronco Gil orders Edgar and Helmuth.

With a pair of clippers, he snips the end of arrow in his shoulder. Santiago thrashes. Edgar Wilson covers his mouth so he won't scream. Old Emetério fetches a bundle of dirty socks and shoves them into the boy's mouth. Bronco Gil starts pulling the arrow by the tip, and little by little it starts to slip. Vladimir holds Santiago's legs firmly in place. He writhes and even before the arrow is fully out, he's passed out on the table. With the piece of the arrow in his hand, Bronco Gil looks closely at the hole it left. He covers the wound with a poultice of herbs and tobacco that he prepares himself.

Edgar Wilson walks around the farm, carrying a mug of freshly-brewed coffee, courtesy of old Emetério. He decides to stretch his legs and gaze at the sky that has just been pierced by daylight, pushing a handful of dark clouds to the edge of the firmament. The sun's rays begin to emerge from behind a mountain and the valley fills with peace. He takes a deep breath, breathing in the damp smell of the dewy morning. It's Sunday, so he mumbles a prayer from his childhood. Edgar Wilson knows that God is in the high places and that He rises every day with the sun. His faith is strong, but he knows his own violence will never allow him to see the face of his Creator. He could redeem himself, but he's never made the effort. His free will leads him in another direction. Edgar Wilson tries to hold onto the image of the sun and its rays emerging at dawn, because he knows that wherever he ends up, he won't see the sun, nor its rays; there will be no dawn, nor the emergence of the Creator. There, it will be like a coal mine, buried in the depths, never seeing the light of day. Two years have gone by and Edgar Wilson still hasn't forgotten the mine where he worked and how that darkness has forever affected him. In a way, he longs for it, to know that in the light of day there is judgment, and that everything lies hidden in the shadows.

He takes a different path back to the dormitory, forcing him to skirt a long-forgotten pond in a part of the farm where they used to raise ducks. But he has never seen a duck since he got there. Feeling worn out and sleepy, Edgar Wilson rubs his stinging eyes as he watches something floating in the pond from a few metres away. He keeps walking at the same pace, fearful of what he will find. He notices there is still some coffee left in the mug and, even though it's cold, he swallows it before bending down at the edge of the water and making the sign of the cross in front of the drowned cow. He picks up a stick and pokes it in vain. He gets up and continues to the dormitory with measured footsteps, demonstrating his peculiar calm. The dead cow cannot be saved. Not even he, who is still alive, can be saved.

Chapter 8

Bronco Gil stands firm in his belief that there is a predator prowling, undetected, along the boundaries of the farm. Milo would like to hire more men to guard the place, but he doesn't have the means.

Since the cow was retrieved from the pond with the help of Vladimir's backhoe, and no bite marks or lacerations were found, everything has returned to apparent normality, but the men have been suspicious about the cattle. Cows don't drown, they don't enter the water unless they're cornered. And this is one of Bronco Gil's lines of thought.

Milo looks up when he hears a soft knock on his open office door and watches Bronco Gil position himself in front of him, his head nearly touching the low plaster ceiling.

'What is it?' says the boss, as he flips through some invoices.

'Senhor Milo, the cows have been behaving well for a week. Every day I perform my checks and none of them have got lost or turned up dead.'

Milo looks pleased, though it is hard to tell through the lines of worry engraved on his face.

'I still don't understand what happened. I thought maybe it was Santiago's fault, scaring the animals away, but after that drowned cow, I don't think he was to blame.'

'Is he better?'

'He's got his nose to the grindstone again. He's a little nutty, but he's hardworking and helpful.'

'Bronco, I want you to keep an eye out.'

'Is there a problem, boss?'

Milo sets the papers on the desk and leans back in his chair. He rubs his ear for a while, silently, before saying:

'I hate to even think it, but I reckon it could be those cattle rustlers who robbed Tapira's place a couple of months back. They never did catch 'em.'

'I hadn't thought of that,' murmurs Bronco Gil.

'I think they might have been the ones who spooked the cows and caused all that ruckus.'

'That's why there weren't any tracks from a predator or nothing,' says Bronco Gil.

'If it was them, they'll be back, don't you think?'

'I suppose so, sir. And I'll be right here waiting for them.'

'Those cattle rustlers have bankrupted a few farms and slaughterhouses to the east. Some of them got arrested, but nothing ever came of it. You know nothing ever comes of these things.'

Milo gets up and takes a rifle from behind a wooden bookcase.

'When I first started my business, I used to stay up all night on watch, running off the chicken thieves. I started my business raising chickens, until one day I bought my first bull.'

Milo sighs, then snaps out of it.

'Did you check that load of sheep?'

'It's all in order. Edgar's already taking care of slaughtering the whole lot. I don't know if he knows how to do the job right.'

'I can't turn away orders,' Milo says, thinking about his obligations to his creditors. 'Give him a hand if it looks like he needs it, but Edgar always manages to get by on his own.' He returns his attention to his desk. Bronco Gil excuses himself and leaves.

A batch of sixty sheep squeezes into a pen away from the others waiting to be taken to slaughter. Their bleating mixes with the lowing of the steer and the heifers, but it is higher pitched and carries farther. Burunga collects some change in his straw hat and is determined to dunk his head in the barrel of water for the third time this week. He almost has all the money he needs for his daughter's glasses. A few more rounds and he'll have scraped together the exact amount. Old Emetério clutches the stopwatch.

'Helmuth, you sure you don't want to change your bet?' asks the old man, smiling with loose dentures.

'I keep my bets, always.'

'What about you, Edgar?'

'I'd rather just watch.'

Burunga leaves the straw hat on the ground with all the coins from the betting and pulls up his trousers, hanging low on his buttocks. He snaps his fingers and takes a breath, filling up with air. He holds on to the sides of the barrel and plunges his big head inside. Five seconds later, he begins to thrash and make bubbles in the water. Those around him laugh at this new performance and cheer him on. Little by little, he begins to still and old Emetério sees that time has gone on too long. Burunga doesn't move a muscle. One of the men touches his back and recoils from the impact.

'He's been electrocuted,' says the man, feeling his hand and arm throb. 'Don't touch him.'

Bronco Gil, who's been observing the whole situation, comes a few steps closer and lassos him, yanking him out of the barrel. Burunga falls dead to the ground, with a frightened look on his face, eyes open and tongue sticking out.

'There's something moving in there,' says Edgar Wilson, looking into the barrel. Helmuth approaches him and the two watch what looks like a snake wiggling in the water.

'It's an eel,' says Edgar Wilson.

'Who the hell put that there?' asks Helmuth.

'I reckon I know who it was,' replies Edgar Wilson.

Santiago approaches the men, distracted and wearing headphones. He sees Burunga lying on the ground and Edgar Wilson and Helmuth beside the barrel. Edgar takes the shotgun slung over Bronco Gil's shoulders and returns to the barrel. As soon as Helmuth flips it over onto the ground, the eel frantically slithers away. Edgar Wilson fires a shot that splits it right in two. Santiago goes pale and places his hand on his chest. Edgar Wilson looks at him and walks towards him.

'Don't you ever bring death from the river into your home or place of work.'

'Is he going to be okay?' asks Santiago.

'That's in God's hands. But for now, he's dead.'

Santiago is distraught. Bronco Gil approaches him:

'I should have wrung your neck when I had the chance,' he growls.

'I just wanted to keep the eel as a pet, I was going to keep it in the abandoned pond.'

'Did you take it to the pond?' asks Bronco Gil.

'I was going to take it today, but I didn't have time, so it was still in the barrel. I thought nobody used that barrel... I thought Burunga only used the other one.' Santiago is almost in tears.

'What did you want a pet electric eel for?' asks Edgar.

'Because I thought it would be fun,' he mutters.

'This guy's got shit for brains,' says old Emetério. 'Ate all that cowshit and now look where it got him. Good for nothing bastard.'

Santiago walks back to the dormitory, distraught, without saying another word. But first, he goes over to Burunga, kneels beside his body, makes the sign of the cross, and apologises. He gathers his belongings and, lying on a bedroll on the floor of the dorm, he waits for the others' decision. Work at the slaughterhouse is partially suspended, as Burunga was the one who oversaw driving the cattle to slaughter. It's not until late afternoon that a police car pulls through the farm gates, followed by a hearse.

Burunga's body is covered with a sheet and candles have been lit around him. Milo is upset, the losses from an unproductive day's work weighing on him.

The men tell the police what happened. They wrap up the two halves of the eel as evidence of the weapon and slide Burunga into the back of the hearse. Santiago is taken to the police station to give his statement, as is Milo, but first Santiago hands Edgar Wilson a bag and gives him a hug:

'Edgar, I'm so sorry,' he says, bowing his head, his heart broken and ashamed.

Santiago gets into the police car and sits in the backseat. Milo follows them in his truck and asks the men to go back to work, saying that no one is to leave, that everybody will have to work through the night, until the sun comes up. Operations at the slaughterhouse cannot be affected by a man's death, as there are still many more head of cattle to be slaughtered. And the sheep must be ready by the end of the next day, when the refrigerated truck will come to pick them up.

After giving his orders, Milo starts up his truck and the cicadas begin to sing. Today there will be no rest, and no sunset on the horizon. Everyone will work overtime.

At the crack of dawn Edgar Wilson is bathed in blood. Each time he went to slaughter one of the sheep, it would kneel in front of him and bow its head in agony. Many of them had tears in their eyes. So, he decided to slit their throats, holding them firmly in his arms and covering their eyes.

He takes a cigarette from the nearly empty packet and lights it with a match. He hadn't eaten anything all day but is unable to feel hungry. He takes just a few sips of coffee. That's all he can stand. The day still shows no signs of arriving, but it will come in an hour and a half, no matter what.

'Edgar.' Helmuth hands him a mug of coffee. Edgar accepts. 'Long goddamn day,' says Helmuth, stretching.

Edgar is silent. He savours the fresh coffee, likely made by old Emetério.

'What an idiot... who keeps an electric eel?' mutters Helmuth. 'Think he'll go to jail? Well, he didn't do it on purpose, I guess. He's just a nutter. I'm sure they'll release him...'

Edgar Wilson remains silent as if he hasn't heard anything. Helmuth calls him by name and shakes him. He notices Edgar is covered in fibres, fur, and blood.

'They kneel down and weep,' says Edgar in a low, drowsy voice.

'What are you talking about?'

'The sheep. They look at you, then kneel down and weep, before they die.'

Edgar Wilson takes a long drag on his cigarette. His lungs fill with smoke, and he releases it slowly from his nostrils.

'I barely made it through. I had to snap some of their necks first, then I'd cover their eyes and slit their throats,' Edgar concludes.

'You need a shower,' says Helmuth.

'What kind of man are you?' asks Edgar Wilson.

'A cattleman.'

They fall silent. Only the gentle sound of the cigarette burning as Edgar inhales can be heard.

'Edgar, they're just animals. They're under our authority.'

'To live or die?'

'To serve us.'

Edgar Wilson stubs out the end of his cigarette on the wooden fence he's leaning against and quietly retreats to the showers. After he cleans himself up, he gets dressed and goes to bed for a bit, as he has two hours of rest before going back to work. He picks up the bag Santiago gave him and finds a few tins of reindeer and elk meat, or so he guesses by the pictures on the labels, and a postcard with a snowy landscape and a wooden bench among tall trees. Everything is covered in ice and gleams with a light he never imagined existed. He'll miss Santiago.

Chapter 9

Edgar Wilson goes back to being the only stun operator at the slaughterhouse. Senhor Milo had promised to hire someone to help out, but he doesn't appear to be in any hurry. Two weeks after Burunga's accidental death, it's as if he'd never been there. One of the butchering employees who had some experience on the job is placed in his role, and the work on the dressing line was shared among the others. Just as cattle resemble one another, the same seems to happen with men. It's difficult to tell them apart. The march of time is like the march of death: it cannot be stopped.

The heifers continue to miscarry their calves, but no cattle go missing or are found dead. Some cows continue to graze to the west, while others remain facing north, as usual. No one seems to mind this small detail, but Edgar Wilson knows that something is still wrong and any normality at the slaughterhouse is in appearance only. He knows this when he watches the cattle grazing, when he looks into their eyes, when he sees his own reflection in them.

The idea of cattle rustlers still lingers, and each morning, at the crack of dawn, Bronco Gil patrols the pastures and the small meat-hanging room. Rustlers steal both cattle and meat. It depends on the gang and how well-equipped they are. But his gut tells him that there are no rustlers hanging about. What happened was not an attempted robbery. There was a kind of disorder, an imbalance that he had never witnessed and cannot explain. He thinks about what Edgar Wilson said when he ruled out there being any predators. He figures he might be right, that the cow had gone mad. That it broke through the fence and dashed itself against the slaughter-house wall because it wanted to.

These are his thoughts as he sits quietly under the guava tree, looking up at the starry sky and the round moon singed with clouds. He is taking a rest after making his second sweep. The pens and pastures are silent. Uggo stands at the ready, roaming in and out of the pastures, nestling in with the cows. Bronco Gil decides to turn in and let the night lull him to sleep like everyone else. He gets up and goes to the dormitory. He throws his shotgun, bow, and arrow to the ground. He takes off his hat, boots, trousers, and braces, and pops out his glass eye, which he keeps inside a cup. He is wearing only boxer shorts and the white T-shirt he usually wears under his plaid shirt. When his body hits the bed, he feels the weight of all those sleepless nights and relaxes deeply, to the lullaby of the other men's snoring and his own grumbling.

A fly lands in Bronco Gil's eye socket. The muscle at the bottom of the hollow twitches. He opens his eye and there is no one else around. He hears some commotion coming from outside. He gets up, knowing he's slept longer than he should have. He puts on his clothes and his boots, and pops his eye in, it goes in crooked, tilted in a way that makes it appear he is looking at his own ear. But the uproar is growing louder, and he decides to go outside before going to the bathroom, not forgetting to sling his shotgun over his shoulder.

'What's going on? Why aren't you all working?' asks Bronco Gil, still sleepy.

Three men argue by the door to the dormitory before answering his question.

'We've been robbed,' one of them says.

Bronco Gil frowns and steps outside and into the daylight, squinting his eye.

'It's one of the pens... it's practically empty,' says another man.

'I think about twenty head have disappeared,' says the third.

Dread coursing through his veins, Bronco Gil feels the need to empty his bladder. He returns ten minutes later with his face washed, his eye straightened and his teeth brushed. Emetério pours him a cup of coffee, and Bronco Gil cracks open the top of a chicken egg by tapping it with his fingernail, making a hole big enough to pour its contents down his throat.

'What do you intend to do?' asks Emetério, in an even huskier voice than usual.

Bronco Gil takes his time to respond and thinks as he savours the last bit of raw egg. Senhor Milo had to go away for a couple of days, to the funeral of his mother-in-law who lived about two hundred kilometres away. In the boss's absence, he's in charge. He doesn't want to lose his job, much less be embarrassed.

'I'm going to find those cows.'

'How you gonna do that?' croaks the old man.

He doesn't answer. He goes to the pen and inspects the broken fence. Tufts of fur, blood and flesh are trapped in the barbed wire. Just like that night the cow broke through the fence, alone. The cattle's hoof prints are scattered everywhere, as if they'd trampled in every direction, but they lead nowhere. At the gate, there are no tyre marks. Transporting twenty-two cows – the exact number of the theft – would take a big truck. There are no footprints on the path leading to the gate. Ultimately, he has the impression that they vanished. He notices that the wooden fence posts are damp, an indication of rain during the night.

He asks the men to go back to work and leaves Tonho armed and on guard. He enters the stun box where Edgar Wilson is getting ready.

'I'm going to need you and Helmuth.'

'Who will slaughter the cattle?'

'Zé Filho can do it.'

'He doesn't have enough experience.'

'He'll manage.'

Edgar takes off his cap and ski goggles.

'We're gonna get those bastards, Edgar. I'm counting on you. Nobody steals from me like that and gets away with it.'

'Do you know who did it?'

'No, but we can't just stand around. I'm going over to Régis Leitão's farm to see if they know anything.'

Bronco Gil hesitates for a moment. He walks around the stun box, taking short steps.

'I heard a while back that he was hauling in stolen cattle. I want to take a look at the place.'

The three men squeeze into the truck. Bronco Gil is at the wheel, Edgar Wilson blows cigarette smoke out the passenger-side window, and Helmuth sits between them, with his dead-fish eyes, awaiting instructions.

They skirt the Rio das Moscas, where a fish kill extending over a large part of the riverbank catches the men's attention. Edgar asks Bronco Gil to stop the vehicle. They get out and approach the fetid pile of fish, some of which are still flopping around. The sun shines down brightly. The sky gleams a glorious shade of blue.

Edgar steps back and stands there looking up to the sky for a few moments, while the other two walk among the dead and dying fish, holding their noses and speculating the reason for such barbaric slaughter.

'I think the water's been poisoned,' says Helmuth.

'It's the blood, that's what's been contaminating the river,' says Bronco Gil, analysing the smell of the water and tasting it with the tip of his tongue. 'It's salty,' he says. He tastes it again and confirms it, shouting: 'The water's salty!'

'But this is a river!' scoffs Helmuth.

'Taste it yourself,' Bronco Gil urges.

Helmuth crouches down and brings a handful of water to his mouth. When he touches the tip of his tongue to the small puddle, his face puckers and he shoots up, terrified.

'It's salty,' he mutters, before repeating himself more loudly.

Edgar Wilson awakens from a moment of contemplation when he hears someone call out his name.

'I've never seen such a thing,' mumbles Bronco Gil, astonished.

'I don't think any fish could survive in there,' says Helmuth.

Edgar Wilson doesn't say a word. He just watches, fearful.

'Death is laying waste to the river,' says Bronco Gil, evoking his ancestors with a little prayer mumbled softly. 'It's like a curse. A very evil spirit walks in these waters,' he concludes.

'Does it have to do with the amount of blood dumped into the river?' asks Helmuth, looking even more disturbed as he finishes the question.

Edgar Wilson lifts his Australian hunting hat and stretches his gaze so far that it seems to meet the fine line that connects the river's murky waters to the sky.

'The river is dead,' says Edgar Wilson, then turns and goes back to the truck. The men just nod their heads in silence before following him.

They continue their journey and an hour later they arrive at Régis Leitão's farm and slaughterhouse. The gate is open. The sign with the name of the farm is lying on the ground. The pickup drives over it, and they head to the loading dock, and park next to a cart with no wheels.

They can tell the place is deserted before they even get out of the vehicle. They walk for ten minutes, each taking a different direction, and it looks like no one has visited the farm for weeks. Inside the slaughterhouse, there are only stray dogs and rats fighting over cattle remains. The pens are empty. A broken tractor rusts in the open surrounded by weeds. In the small dorm, there are only a few rags on the floor, cigarette butts and empty bottles of booze. Bronco Gil tries the doorknob to Régis Leitão's office and sees that it is locked.

The three men reconvene in the loading and unloading yard, looking more confused than when they first arrived.

'It must be at least a month since anybody's set foot here,' says Helmuth.

'What the hell is going on?' murmurs Bronco Gil. 'I never heard about them closing the place.'

'Well, they don't have our cows,' says Edgar Wilson.

'The office is locked,' says Bronco Gil. 'I think we'd better take a look inside.'

Edgar Wilson grabs a crowbar from the slaughter-house and the three men head to the office. They break down the door and a statue of São Roque, sitting on a small shelf above the door frame, crashes to the floor, barely missing Edgar's nose. It feels like a bad omen. They enter carefully. The musty odour is disgusting, but they see nothing suspicious or that indicates the slaughter-house has closed. Edgar Wilson picks up the pieces of the saint from the ground and puts them on the desk, and the three men leave, feeling suffocated.

Back in the yard, they stand in silence, pensive. They separate again, looking for clues or debris that might point to what happened. Half an hour later, they are back together and feeling defeated.

The sky turned grey an hour ago and heavy clouds hang over the region. After a few claps of thunder, they climb into the truck and a hard rain catches them on the way back.

Only the driver's side windshield wiper is working. Because of the poor visibility, Edgar Wilson had insisted on driving. The wind and rain grow stronger as they travel along the deserted road. A fallen tree forces Edgar Wilson to make a detour, turning off the main road and taking an alternate route, ill-advised on a rainy day due to all the potholes, slippery mud, and the sharp drop-off, with no guard rail. Edgar has taken this route several times and whenever he can, he gets out of the car to look down at Rio das Moscas from above, a commanding view on sunny days.

'I think we should stop,' says Helmuth. 'Rain's coming down too hard.'

Edgar agrees to stop as soon as he finds a conducive spot set back from the road, but before that happens one of the rear tyres gets stuck. They get out to push the truck.

'Let's just leave it here and stay under the trees,' says Helmuth.

'Another car might come,' yells Edgar Wilson, soaking wet, his voice muffled by thunder. 'We need to move the truck out of the way.'

Bronco Gil picks up a log and places it under the

tyre, and as he and Edgar Wilson push, Helmuth presses the accelerator, but they're unable to shift the vehicle from where it sits.

It starts to rain even harder, and the mud turns into a slippery soup making their feet sink deeper and deeper. The stretch of road they are on is a gentle descent, but under these circumstances, there is no friction between the tyre and the ground and the truck threatens to slide off the cliff.

'It's not working,' shouts Edgar, smeared with mud.

Bronco Gil wants to try one more time and they push the truck again. It starts to move slowly. Edgar Wilson puts his weight on the log to give the tyre more stability, but this only causes it to slither to the side, tipping towards the cliff edge. They yell for Helmuth to get out of the vehicle, and he jumps into a puddle just in time, grabbing hold of some weeds just before the truck topples over the cliff and crashes down below.

The three men just stand there, paralysed. Lightning strikes a nearby tree. Helmuth gets up and tries not to look back at the drop. Edgar Wilson walks slowly to the edge of the cliff and plants his feet on a rough piece of rock that supports his weight. He looks down and sees the riverbank, the one opposite the road they usually travel. Bronco Gil yells for him to get back and take cover under a tree, even though it's dangerous. It's a remarkable amount of rain, and unusual for this time of year.

Edgar Wilson does not respond to Bronco Gil's calls and stands staring at the precipice, becoming nothing but a silhouette in the deluge. He motions for Bronco Gil and Helmuth to join him. They hesitate. Edgar insists.

'What are you doing, Edgar? Get out of there,' yells Bronco Gil.

'I found them,' Edgar Wilson replies.

'Found what?' yells Bronco Gil.

Another bolt of lightning makes Bronco Gil and Helmuth retreat, and Edgar Wilson raises his hands over his head, protecting himself.

'I found them,' Edgar Wilson insists.

'Edgar, do you want to get hit by lightning? Get out of there now!' orders Bronco Gil.

'I found them,' shouts Edgar Wilson insistently, waving.

'What did you find, Edgar?' asks Helmuth.

'Come see,' says Edgar Wilson.

Bronco Gil walks carefully, his boots sinking in the mire, followed by Helmuth, who uses a tree branch as a staff. They approach Edgar, who is staring down the precipice.

'What is it, Edgar?' Bronco Gil shouts angrily.

'I found them,' he replies, pointing down. Bronco Gil and Helmuth look down, and at the very bottom of the precipice are the twenty-two cows and the pickup truck, smashed, on the banks of the Rio das Moscas.

'Getting stuck here was a sign,' says Edgar Wilson.

'Cows don't jump off cliffs,' says Bronco Gil.

'And rivers don't turn salty overnight,' Edgar Wilson retorts. 'We're only one kilometre from the slaughter-house. They walked here.'

'Or were brought here,' says Helmuth.

Edgar Wilson is startled by a clap of thunder and slips. Bronco Gil grabs him by the shirt and Helmuth helps him hold on. Edgar begins to slide back, and Bronco Gil grabs the rope he keeps around his waist, slips it under Edgar Wilson's arms and tugs, helped by Helmuth. The two can't find anything to brace their feet against and they dance around in the mud for a while until they manage to pull Edgar up. They catch their breath, and move back under the canopy, where they wait for the rain to pass, without uttering a single word to one another.

Chapter 10

In the early evening, a load of cattle arrives at the slaughterhouse by truck. This time it doesn't take long for the local hungry to cross the gate in pursuit. It had been a very hard day, but luckily the production line had operated normally. Only a few head of cattle needed to be slaughtered that day, and the heaviest work was left to the butchering, gutting and deboning staff. Stepping into the slaughterhouse, Helmuth hurried to check the condition of the chainsaw and found that it had been used correctly and that the carcasses had been split symmetrically. He was relieved.

The shipment was expected at the crack of dawn, but the driver explained that they'd had to travel further afield to pick up another load to be taken to a different slaughterhouse. The fence surrounding the empty pen, which once housed the missing cows, is broken in several places. Their solution was to cram the herd of thirty-five head of cattle into an old barn at the back of the slaughterhouse. Tonho repairs the fence with the help of old Emetério, but they'll only be able to finish the job in the morning, by daylight.

Bronco Gil fires two shots into the air, which sets the women and children, hungry for a rejected cow, running.

He locks the gate, picks up the sign with the name of the slaughterhouse that has fallen on the ground and hangs it up again. He sees that it's crooked and adjusts it until it looks straight to him. He returns to the farm, lugging his shotgun, still warm from firing, and is saddened by the thought of scaring off dogs and people in the same manner. Like Edgar Wilson, Bronco Gil still cultivates some deep, hidden sentiment for his fellow man, even though most of the time he feels more of a fellowship with animals.

'I want both of you on watch with me tonight.' Bronco Gil points to Edgar Wilson and Helmuth. 'Nobody's getting any shuteye. Let's get those bastards.'

'Why would anybody tip the cows over the cliff?' asks Edgar Wilson. 'If they're rustlers they ought to sell them to some other slaughterhouse.'

'Maybe something went wrong, I don't know,' says Bronco Gil. 'But somebody herded them there. Senhor Milo will be arriving back late tomorrow morning and I want to show him we caught those thieves.'

It's past midnight and the three men are on watch in the cattle pens. Some mooing is heard from time to time from inside the old wooden barn. The cows that will be slaughtered in the morning have only water to feed on, the same water diet for all cattle.

It starts to drizzle in the wee hours, and the temperature drops slightly, creating a pleasant feeling in the valley. Uggo stays at the ready with the three men and occasionally leaves the pens and goes to the old wooden barn.

The place where the cows fell is inaccessible to any type of vehicle. Even by water it's dangerous, there are rocks at the bottom of the river, which would smash the hull of any boat that came near. That side of the riverbank is nothing more than the formation of an abyss, a giant sinkhole in the earth, created only to enter and not to leave. No way out.

Bronco Gil, moving restlessly from one side to the other, smokes his pipe in silence. Edgar Wilson is leaning against the fence of one of the pens, drinking a cup of coffee to ward off sleep. Helmuth walks among the cattle and sometimes wanders off to spy on possible access points to the farm.

When the drizzle turns into a light but constant rain, Edgar Wilson takes shelter under the guava tree and Helmuth follows him. Bronco Gil remains in place with his pipe lit, and the ember doesn't go out, not even in the rain.

Edgar Wilson had left the bag with the tinned meats under the guava tree. He sits down on the stump and with a can opener removes the lid from the potted moose meat. He scoops some out with two fingers and brings it to his mouth. The taste is strong, but he quickly gets used to it. He clicks his tongue when swallowing. Helmuth tries it but doesn't like it. He takes off his hat and sits it on his thighs. He rests the shotgun against the trunk they're sitting on and leans back against the tree.

'That Indian sure is obsessed,' says Helmuth. 'People say he's killed some fifty men. After he kills them, he scalps them. They say he keeps all the scalps after he lets them dry in the sun for several days. But I think there's more legend than truth in Bronco Gil's story.'

'How'd he lose his eye?' asks Edgar.

'He got run over. I think he's slowing down now. Running out of steam, or something.'

Uggo barks repeatedly and the sound comes from the direction of the old barn where the newly arrived cows are. Edgar Wilson and Helmuth get up and run towards the old barn after Bronco Gil, who has shot off in the direction of Uggo's barking. At first there is nothing unusual, but at the back of the barn, the narrow and poorly secured door offers passage to the cows who, one by one, in the rain, are unhurriedly trotting toward one of the farm boundaries. Edgar Wilson and Helmuth stop right behind Bronco Gil and stand there watching.

'Is someone guiding them?' Helmuth asks quietly.

Bronco Gil, binoculars raised, says he doesn't see anyone. Helmuth takes the binoculars.

'But where are they going?' asks Helmuth when he sees there is no one driving the cattle.

'They're going to the cliff on that side there,' says Edgar Wilson.

'How do you know?' asks Bronco Gil.

'That's where I'd go.'

The three men decide to just watch the cattle's quiet movement and, when they've all left the barn, they follow them from a distance. The first cow jumps and then the second. Bronco Gil tries to put a stop to it, but is blocked by Edgar and Helmuth, who have decided to just watch the horrific spectacle. And so the cattle keep jumping, one after the other, until all of them have leapt over the edge, emitting long moos.

They peer down from the edge of the cliff but see nothing. Only in the morning, when the sun comes up, are they able to survey the collective suicide.

'They were fleeing the predator,' says Bronco Gil.

'There were no predators,' snaps Helmuth gruffly.

'You still don't get it, do you Helmuth? Don't you understand who the predator is?' says Bronco Gil, glaring at him.

He looks down again, into the darkness below, and sighs as he begins to understand it in the others' silence.

'What do you think, Edgar?' asks Helmuth.

'One abyss calling out to another abyss.' Edgar Wilson's eyes reflect the unfathomable darkness always present in the ruminants' eyes.

Back at the dormitory they tossed and turned in their beds but couldn't sleep. They are anxious for dawn and for the task they will have before them. They are the first to get up; and under the day's first rays of sun, they head to the cliff. The entire herd of cows is in a heap. In the distance, they hear Milo's pickup and decide to go talk to him, even though they hesitate to tell what happened, to truly believe what they witnessed. They knock on the office door and file in, holding their hats. With the three of them crammed together inside the small room, it's hard to think and breathe at the same time.

'So, how'd everything go?' asks Milo, appearing somewhat refreshed.

'First of all, sir, we want to offer our condolences on the death of your mother-in-law,' says Bronco Gil.

'God rest her soul,' says Milo with a grin. 'My wife is beside herself, but for me it was a relief. That old woman cost me dearly. I had to cover all the expenses. I think now I might even be able to trade that old truck for a new one.'

Milo hears his own excitement and clears his throat, adopting a certain composure, attempting to show some grief.

'Something happened that…' begins Bronco Gil.

Immediately his grief becomes real and his heart races.

'Sir, I don't know how to say this…'

'Spit it out!' shouts Milo.

Bronco Gil stammers. He takes a deep breath.

'The cows from the last shipment died,' says Edgar Wilson.

'Tapira's cows? What do you mean they died? Died

where, how?' asks Milo, his eyes wide with fear.

'They jumped off the cliff,' says Edgar Wilson.

'What? What are you talking about, Edgar?' shouts Milo.

'It's true, Senhor Milo,' says Helmuth. 'Tapira's cows jumped off a cliff in the middle of the night.'

'Cows don't kill themselves. We're the ones who kill them,' bellows Milo.

From the top of the cliff, the four men look down on the deathly scene.

'They jumped, one at a time,' says Helmuth.

'You didn't do anything?' asks Milo, heavy-hearted.

'There was nothing we could do,' says Edgar Wilson.

'You idiots could have stopped them,' insists their boss.

'Senhor Milo, there's one more thing,' says Bronco Gil.

'More? There's more?' bellows Milo.

'Yesterday during the day, we went out to look for a group of twenty-two cows from our herd and they were lying in a chasm a kilometre from here. Total loss,' concludes Bronco Gil.

Milo steps back from the edge of the cliff. He ambles a few steps away and feels a pounding in his chest. He rubs his eyes and wipes his neck and face with a grimy washcloth. After a few minutes of silence, he asks:

'Is it something to do with those Lebanese cows?'

'I very much doubt it, sir,' replies Bronco Gil.

'This is a big loss. What am I going to tell Tapira? I've never heard of such a thing happen. Never seen anything like it.'

'I think we'd better reinforce the fences and put two men to watch each pen,' says Helmuth.

Milo nods silently and asks: 'Do you have any idea what happened?'

The men shake their heads. Milo dismisses them and asks Bronco Gil to report the incident to the other cowhands and to call Vladimir to come remove the cows with his backhoe, which will probably be several days' work. In this spot, it's possible to get in on foot or with a vehicle. The herd must be removed before the dead meat starts to attract vultures and the stench becomes unbearable.

Edgar Wilson is turning to leave when he hears Milo calling him.

'What do you think happened, Edgar?'

'They killed themselves.'

'Edgar, they're just animals. They have no free will. They don't think about suicide.'

'I think they've grown fond of us.'

Milo looks out over the cliff. The horizon is aglow, and the sun is partially risen behind the mountains, peeking out in golden rays. All the weight on Milo's face vanishes. He takes a deep breath and, for a brief moment, feels peace. A small peace, but sensitive to his spirit.

Chapter 11

It is early afternoon and Vladimir is standing on the cliff's edge, his mouth open, staring down.

'Holy moly!' He makes the sign of the cross on his chest. 'Those cows have put you out of a job, Edgar.'

'Senhor Milo's going to reinforce the fences and he won't be taking any new shipments until it's done.'

Vladimir mentally plots a path for the best way in to collect the cows with the backhoe. They notice some people going in, surrounding the dead cattle. Another group approaches in a cart.

'They beat the vultures here,' says Vladimir.

'It's going to be hard to stop them from loading up the cows,' says Edgar Wilson.

'We'd better hurry.'

Edgar Wilson climbs into the backhoe with Vladimir, and they proceed to the collection point. About twenty people, including men, women, and children, are butchering the cows with hatchets. Some men stand in their way, blocking the backhoe from going any further.

'You ain't coming in here,' says one of the men.

'These cattle are spoken for,' says Vladimir. 'I need to collect them.'

'The cows jumped from up above. Our prayers have been answered,' says another man in the group, holding a hatchet.

'These cows are under the charge of Senhor Milo,' Vladimir argues.

'You'll go no further. We're taking all the cattle.' The man raises his hatchet.

Vladimir turns off the backhoe and steps down with Edgar Wilson. They look closely at the carcasses. A pickup truck parks a few metres away and a group of men and women get out of the back and run towards the cattle.

'We won't be able to remove any of them,' Vladimir says.

Senhor Milo and Bronco Gil approach the two men. They sense the commotion at the scene.

'I called the cops,' says Milo. 'They're coming over to file a report.'

'They better get here soon, otherwise there won't be any evidence left,' says Bronco Gil.

Before long there are more than fifty people butchering the dead cattle, gathering body parts and piling them onto wagons, pickup trucks and bicycles. Those without tools drag pieces across the ground in nylon or canvas bags.

There's nothing to be done but sit and watch. The vultures await any viscera dropped on the ground, scraps left by the dogs.

It is already late afternoon when two police officers finally arrive. By then only the vultures remain, fighting over a chunk of tripe or piece of skin, sinking into pools of blood. They immediately ask about the dead cows.

'Without the bodies we can't write a report.'

'A mob took everything, ransacked the corpses,' Milo protests.

Vultures circle overhead, screeching. The officer in charge of writing the report looks to the sky and says,

'Too pretty a day for there to be so many vultures in the sky. How many cows?'

'Thirty-five,' replies Bronco Gil.

'What a coincidence!' the policeman says with a grin. 'Tomorrow I'll be married thirty-five years. We're going to have a barbecue.' When he finishes, he clears his throat and spits out the phlegm. 'Write that down,' he orders the younger officer who accompanies him.

'Well, officer, where does that leave us?' asks Milo.

'Without the cows, or rather without the bodies, I can't write the report.'

'I understand, sir, but this herd wasn't mine. I've got to answer to the owner,' insists Milo, trying to argue in the most cordial way he knows how.

'I'll report them as missing,' says the officer.

'A whole crew of men and women just left here with the cows in pieces,' says Milo. 'All you have to do is open an investigation, sir. Those people have never had so much meat in their homes.'

'We don't have enough men to do a search like that. Did anyone see what happened? How did they fall?'

'They jumped,' says Helmuth.

The policeman is silent for a moment. He looks to the top of the cliff. He crouches down next to the vultures and pokes at the remains of some entrails with a stick, his shoes in pools of blood.

'They jumped off – on their own?' asks the policeman.

'That's right. They just jumped,' says Helmuth.

'I once had a cat that threw itself into a river. Never did understand that. It leapt off my lap and just jumped in the river. I tried to save it, but an alligator was faster than me. I mourn its death to this day. Never wanted nothing to do with cats ever again.'

They stand in silence for some time just listening to the croaking vultures.

'Well, it's evident there's been a tragedy here. I can tell that from the amount of blood. Can we say the cattle slipped and fell off the cliff? I think that's quite possible.'

The men exchange glances. They hesitate to agree with the officer.

'Look, if I say the cows jumped of their own volition, it's going to sound pretty odd, don't you think? Better to put accidental death followed by theft of the corpses. I'll use all that blood as evidence of the accident and the crime of looting, what do you think? It's the best I can do.'

Senhor Milo, crestfallen and defeated, agrees. The story is absurd, and he doesn't want to become a laughingstock. Either way, his slaughterhouse will be affected, at least for a few months, until he can regain the trust of his customers. As for the dead cattle, he will have to replace them from his own herd and hope that Tapira will accept the deal, as that way he won't have any losses.

The police officer says goodbye and leaves with the younger officer.

'I don't think he believed us,' says Bronco Gil.

'I don't buy that cat story,' says Helmuth.

'Me neither,' agrees Edgar Wilson.

'That's what we're going to say, that the cows fell, that it was an accident,' says Milo.

'And the other herd, that fell onto the banks of the Rio das Moscas?' asks Edgar Wilson.

'We'll say the same thing,' says Milo.

'Are they gonna believe it?' asks Bronco Gil.

'I don't know, Bronco. But what can we say? That the cattle are cursed?' says the boss. 'Let's leave it at that and keep a lid on it.'

'Régis Leitão's farm shut down,' said Edgar Wilson. 'They abandoned everything.'

'I heard they got looted several times,' says Milo.

'Maybe they got looted the same way the cows accidentally fell off that cliff,' adds Edgar Wilson.

Milo looks at him. He has that same haunting impression that Edgar Wilson knows more than he says. That he can sense the earth's magnetic field the way ruminants do.

'Think things will get back to normal?' murmurs Bronco Gil.

'I hope so,' says Milo fearfully.

They return to the slaughterhouse and avoid talking about it with the other workers. All they say is it was an accident.

The next morning, before slaughtering a few head of cattle, Edgar Wilson notices that the cows in the pasture are all facing north, chewing grass, swatting flies with their tails, and keeping their normal, everyday pace.

Once again, blood is shed each day. In a few months, production will ramp up due to a new meat-packing plant for hamburgers and other beef products near the slaughterhouse. Milo will finally be able to buy that new pickup truck and even renovate the dormitory, whose roof was partially damaged during a storm, which is why the men now sleep under the stars.

Edgar Wilson continues his sign of the cross and lime ritual until a new stun operator is hired. He's been ready to leave ever since he was offered a job at the hog farm. His days with ruminants are over.

The cattle's collective suicide would remain un-explained. Perhaps it was Divine Providence answering the prayers of the local residents who begged for food, especially meat. Just as the Israelites were met with a shower of quail, people of other deserts received a shower of cattle: meat from the heavens; death that gives life.

After gathering his belongings, Edgar stops by Senhor Milo's office to collect his pay for his final weeks of work. He shakes the boss's hand and thanks him for the job and for the trust placed in him all this time. Milo feels his chest tighten. Edgar is his best employee. He'll miss him.

Edgar Wilson puts on his hat and climbs into the truck that had brought those men to work in the slaughterhouse.

'Where you headed, son?' asks the driver as they head towards the farm gate.

'I'm going west, to work with hogs.'

The driver nods. There's a cool breeze in the new day, and the smell of damp vegetation.

'Got tired of the job?'

'Yeah, I got tired.'

'Before I bought this truck and started working with freight, I slaughtered cattle, too. Miserable work. Pays a pittance.'

Edgar Wilson asks if he can smoke and lights a cigarette. He offers one to the driver, who accepts it and tucks it behind his ear.

'The whole day I'd be covered in blood. Stank all the time. My wife could smell carrion as soon as I stepped through the front door.' The driver chuckles. He pauses to think before continuing and sighs: 'It really was disgusting.'

Ahead of them a procession brings the truck to a crawl. They pass slowly among men, women and children. Edgar Wilson recognises a few faces, some of those who carried the dead cattle from the cliff.

'I don't know what they're so grateful for. They have nothing. This here is a desert.'

'Maybe they have something to be thankful for this time around,' says Edgar Wilson.

They cross through the procession, and the driver hits the accelerator to make the truck go as fast as it can.

They pass by the construction site of the new hamburger and meat-packing plant.

'We're getting another factory,' says the driver, his voice flat, looking slightly annoyed. 'It's going to be a big one.'

'There's going to be plenty of work to go around,' says Edgar Wilson.

'Yes, son, plenty to go around. Like they say in these parts: as long as there's a cow in this world, there will be a man keen to kill it.'

'And another keen to eat it,' concludes Edgar Wilson.

The driver smirks and grabs the cigarette from behind his ear. Edgar Wilson strikes a match and lights it. The man thanks him.

'There'll always be a bunch of people willing to eat it. But not to kill it. Only folks like you and me, boy. Only folks like us.'

Now and again, the glare from the sun dazzles the driver's vision, who squints his eyes. A hot day, a terribly hot day. By nightfall, Edgar Wilson will be at his new job, meeting the hogs and listening to their grunts. He knows his predatory days are not over and shedding blood will still be his means of survival. It's what he knows how to do. Maybe one day he'll find another job, one that's clean. For now, he'll keep slaughtering hogs; impure but morally acceptable, that's how he feels. There is no one to stop him, for men like him, slaughterers, are few and far between. Those who eat are many, and they are never satiated. They are all men of blood, those who kill and those who eat. No one goes unpunished.

Final Note

'In any case civilisation has made mankind if not more blood-thirsty, at least more vilely, more loathsomely blood-thirsty... Now we do think bloodshed abominable and yet we engage in this abomination, and with more energy than ever.'

Fyodor Dostoyevsky, *Notes from Underground*
(trans. Constance Garnett)

CHARCO PRESS

Director & Editor: Carolina Orloff
Director: Samuel McDowell

www.charcopress.com

Of Cattle and Men was published on
90gsm Munken Premium Cream paper.

The text was designed using Bembo 11.5 and ITC Galliard.

Printed in December 2022 by TJ Books
Padstow, Cornwall, PL28 8RW using responsibly
sourced paper and environmentally-friendly adhesive.